SHORT
STORIES

The Stuntman's Daughter
and Other Stories

The Stuntman's Daughter
and Other Stories

by
Alice Blanchard

University of North Texas Press
Denton, Texas

5 4 3 2 1

Requests for permission to reproduce material from this
work should be sent to:

Permissions
University of North Texas Press
PO Box 13856
Denton TX 76203

The paper used in this book meets the minimum requirements of the
American National Standard for Permanence of Paper for Printed
Library Materials, Z39.48.1984.

Library of Congress Cataloging-in-Publication Data

Blanchard, Alice.
    The stuntman's daughter : stories / by Alice Blanchard.
        p. cm.
    "Winner, Katherine Anne Porter prize in short fiction, Rick
DeMarinis, judge."
    ISBN 1-57441-009-1
    1. Manners and customs—Fiction. I. Title.
PS3552.L36512S78   1996
813'.54—dc20   95-26177
                                                          CIP

For Doug, with love.

Table of Contents

Claybottom Lake—1

The Stuntman's Daughter—11

Annabelle—21

Blindfold—35

The Boarder—51

Americans—67

The Accident Radio—77

Messages—91

Corporation Beach—105

The Blue Pontiac—119

Puddle Tongue—137

Acknowledgements—155

Claybottom Lake

I am the father of three daughters and stepfather to a fourth. Nola's out behind the pottery shed right now, throwing rocks at the paper wasps that make their home beneath the eaves. She squeals with excitement each time a wasp dips and curls around her head; no doubt, she'll be wailing soon as one of them lands a nasty sting. Nola is a tomboy, a hell-raiser, a maverick, and she's captured my heart like no other. She's got the broad choppy legs of an athletic boy and the scowl of an old maid. No matter how many baths she takes, she manages to smell unwashed. She stands in the sunlight, an amber specimen in a glass jar, still as an Indian or a stone. Then quick as an insect, she sparks into action, running down the hill where the wasps won't follow, stepping on the dried brown grass.

She sees me watching her and frowns. There is a hostility in my stepdaughter's eyes that is different from the hostility in my three daughters' eyes; Nola looks at me with the cool indifference of a paper wasp making lazy dives in the hot summer air.

Nola is nothing like my other daughters. Together they form a dark and light threesome—a blend of pinks and whites, blues and browns—too shy to hate me outright. Three slender, pale adolescents who watch me from their mother's house with a special curiosity. Each of them has loved me, and I have loved all of them. I've bought them birthday presents and cleaned the vomit from their hair. They've planted wet kisses on my face and given me gifts of wilted wild flowers. Charlie, the youngest, used to go fishing with me, carrying the poles like a soldier on a mission. She'd wrinkle up

1

her nose as she slid the thick worms onto the fish hooks. Now they stick together, forming a silent watchful group that goes from house to shiny blue VW Rabbit back to house again.

Sometimes I imagine they exist simply to prick my conscience. In a blistering dream, they are three devils casting evil spells on me. My girls, forming a watery line through the garden, take a shortcut down the hill to their own private beach by the lake. Their heads bob gently on their gooselike necks and their thin bodies remind me of a colt's legs, so slender and ungainly and in synch with each other they are.

I live about fifty feet from my ex-wife's house, just fifty feet from my three watchful daughters, in the pottery studio where I've earned my living for the past 15 years. Behind the studio gallery where ceramics are displayed, behind the drafty room where I throw my pots and set them out to dry, behind the kilns in which the stoneware bakes, I've built a small apartment—two narrow rooms and a kitchenette and bathroom. After the divorce, it was decided I should stay here so that I can continue to pay alimony and child-support. It hasn't been easy, let me tell you. My ex-wife's family lives up the street, and every day I endure the death-threat stares of my former in-laws as they pass by in their Lincoln Continental.

We live near Claybottom Lake in a small Cape Cod town. I sell pottery to tourists every spring and summer. During the winter months, I teach Ceramics at a local college and lecture at state universities. I am fairly well-known for my skills with clay. I've even invented a new glaze, Claybottom Crystal, a blend of five different powders. My second wife, Mae, teaches biology at the college. Early mornings, she explains my anatomy to me, pointing out my different organs, rolling her ringed fingers over my softening muscles. We were married last February, and now it is June, and Nola still hasn't spoken to me. Not one word. When it comes to me, her lips are as sealed as the flap of a licked envelope.

"Be careful!" I call out to her, and she curls her fingers inward, the tips touching, as if I've caught her in the middle of some embarrassing, private act. "They'll sting more than once, y'know. They're not like bees. Bees lose their stingers and die. They've only got one chance, but wasps are vicious. They'll sting you a dozen times. They've got nothing to lose."

She gazes at me as if I've lost my wits, and perhaps I have? I am about to adopt her. I stand shirtless, my tan pot belly hanging over my belt buckle like a bowl of yeasty dough. She stares at me until I feel like a complete fool and then, as if I've ruined her game, she turns and stumbles down the hill, her yellow flip-flops farting rhythmically. She wears a solid yellow dress that captures patches of sunlight from between the trees and throws it back to me in brilliant flashes of light. Nola is a strobing firefly, my own private fireworks, the glinting windshield of a car weaving through heavy traffic. Her dusty hair comes down to her shoulders and curves over the rough pink skin.

She has defeated me again.

My three daughters, full of bitterness over the divorce, still love me. My ex-wife, protected from me by her angry parents and efficient lawyer, used to love me. Mae loves me dearly. I am spoiled by the easygoing love of the women in my life, and suddenly I realize I will not rest until Nola loves me, too.

Mae is a patient woman, slightly domineering, with thin lips and almond eyes. When we were married, five months ago, she had a model's figure. Since then she's gained about 15 pounds, and I'm amazed at the way her thighs pour from her hips, liquid white as bone. I take great pleasure in kneading her flesh, which is so much like raw clay when it's set to harden in the sun; I smell my fingers afterward, damp with her scent. I call her my Earth mother, because there is so much of her now, intending it as a compliment, but she melts into tears. She hates being fat, she says. She's afraid I will stop loving her. But how could I stop loving a woman who pores over pictures of dissected animals? A woman whose head is full of terms like "lymphatic ducts" and "intercostal glands"? How could I stop loving a woman who presents me with a picture of the muscles of the female perinaeum as a sexual overture? A woman who pulls at her lower lip until all the lipstick is rubbed off? A woman who uses the full range and pitch of her voice to get her message across? A woman who sprinkles Old Spice under her arms instead of deodorant? Tell me, how?

Mae has taken the summer off and is teaching Nola to swim. Nola, big for her age, grumbles about the too-tight bathing suit, the yucky bathing cap, water in her ears. Still, Mae is determined that her daughter will learn to swim. They stand beside me, arguing, and I pretend not to listen as I bend over my pottery wheel and raise a wet column from a revolving lump of stoneware.

"There's ocean all around us," Mae says, and Nola wrinkles her nose and stares at the floor, kicking up pink clouds of clay dust. "We live near a lake now. I don't want you to drown."

"I wouldn't drown if I never went in," Nola grumbles. "You're the one who's making me go in. I'd never go in and I'd never drown if it wasn't for you."

I stay out of their way, just as I stayed out of my ex-wife's way when she and the three girls fought. I couldn't keep up with their barrage of words. Words upon words, like heaped layers of dirt. And Sybil's viciousness, the things she called them! I was as frightened of her venom as they were.

But these fights between Nola and Mae are different—strange and gentle negotiations. No shrill accusations, no bitterness here, just Mae's reasoned queries and Nola's terse replies.

"Go put your new bathing suit on. I want to see how it fits."

"I'll put the suit on," Nola says, "but I won't go in the water. I'll wear the stupid suit, but I'm not going swimming!" Then she runs out back to her small bedroom and Mae throws me an anguished look.

"Sam," she says, "say something. Don't just sit there, support me on this."

"She won't talk to me," I tell her, pulling the spinning clay, wetting it with a sponge and molding the lip of a new vase.

After several minutes, Nola stumbles in, stubbing her toe on the base of the potter's wheel and swearing, bending over to pick the lint from between her toes, showing me her derriere. She's gained some weight, like her mother, and the suit—a dark blue maillot—is ill-fitting. Nola, a 12-year-old in a growing body, resents having to show me anything, especially her pale fleshy arms and the scraggly blonde hairs covering her muscled legs.

"Turn around, Nola," Mae says excitedly. "Isn't she pretty?"

"I don't want to turn around."

"Turn around, sweetheart! Show Sam how pretty you look."

"I won't turn around," she says calmly, quietly. End of discussion.

I don't look long, just nod my approval and go back to work, holding a piece of wire taut between my fingers and slicing the vase from the wheel with one swift motion.

✳

After Nola came to live with us, I worked hard to get her to open up. She has never spoken to me, not directly. She's never said my name out loud. In order to gain her affection, I have done all sorts of stepfatherly things: I buy her ice-cream sundaes, put toads in jelly jars and punch air holes in the lids, give her my spare change, nickel-and-dime bribes. I've been teaching her how to use clay. I hand her wooden carving tools and a lump of my best porcelain—smooth, unblemished, wet gray. I explain that porcelain lightens as it dries; once it's fired in the kiln, it'll turn white as snow. She fools around, pounding the clay flat with her fist, pinching its edges to make an ashtray. She never looks at me directly, lowers her eyes whenever I come near.

On Thursday, I give her some clay, and she makes a hamburger patty, two buns, a couple of french fries. Quite imaginative, I think, spreading the pieces over a narrow shelf to dry. They'll be bisqued, glazed and fired, I tell her.

The next day, Mae and I take a drive up north, visit different beaches and watch the wet rollings of the Atlantic. We leave Nola alone for the afternoon. She has the run of the house, plenty of food to eat, and color TV. Mae and I make love on the strange-smelling bed of a cheap motel, and she cries out against my fevered humping, no longer inhibited by a young daughter in the next room.

When we return home, Mae takes Nola out for pizza, and I set to work on some bisqueware that needs glazing. I discover Nola's hamburger and french fries smashed in a corner of the studio, along with two of my recently thrown casseroles. The clay, still moist, holds her toeprints. I decide not to mention the incident to Mae; I don't want to upset her. I don't say anything to Nola, either. I figure she is leaving me a message—her anger, mashed and rumpled in a corner of the dusty floor. Her creativity and mine—dropped, tromped on, crushed to a powdery white dust. I don't say a word to anyone, just sweep up the debris and dump it.

Later that night, I tiptoe into Nola's room and sit on the edge of her bed. She is watching me expectantly, her eyes bright in the semidark.

"Thanks for letting your mom and me have the afternoon to ourselves," I say, sweat trickling down my neck. "Next time, we'll make sure to bring you along."

She says nothing, her eyes narrowing critically, and when I bend to kiss her cheek, she jerks away. I kiss the hair over her ear instead. As I tiptoe out, I have the lousy feeling I've failed another of her tests.

※

"Nola, where are you going?" I say. She has rushed through the studio in her blue bathing suit, accidentally knocking some sales receipts off my desk. As she hurries away, I decide I've had enough of her silence, her stony stares. I follow her down the embankment to Claybottom Lake.

There are several private beaches on this side of the lake and, since the divorce, I've used a neighbor's. It's a tiny beach, not much bigger than Nola's room. The sand is covered with pine needles, and the lake bottom is so murky, your feet sink deeper with each step. Tadpoles by the hundreds bask in the shallows between stiff ashen reeds. Go a short distance and the bottom drops abruptly, the lake grows cold and still as the basement of a museum.

I follow Nola down the coiling path. She knows I am behind her but doesn't look around; her irritation is written in the jerking of her spine, the knuckling of her shoulders. I can't believe she hates me so much. I'm a simple man, a potter. I make a decent living. I never meant to leave my first wife; it just happened. Things became intolerable. We had irreconcilable differences. We fell pathetically out of love with one another.

I wonder what it is that Nola needs to hear? That I love her and her mother dearly? That she won't always have to live here and endure the hardened stares of my three daughters? That someday soon we'll have a house of our own? That she doesn't have to learn to swim this summer?

"Nola," I say gently, so as not to alarm her, "mind if I come with you?" A stupid question, but what else do you say to a voluntary mute?

She shrugs, not bothering to look back. I could be the wind or a groping tree branch for all she cares. She watches so much TV, Mae is afraid she'll have commercials between her dreams. She plays dangerous games, draws treasure maps and burns the edges for authenticity, drops the spent matches in her metal wastebasket. She spends hours alone in the woods. She didn't make any new friends at her new school last year. She rides her bike around the circular driveway in front of my ex-wife's house, alarming the dog with her gravel-spitting swerves. She grits her teeth and pretends to be a Hell's Angel. She sucks in breath and blows on her thumb until she crumples in a dead faint. She loves bats and horror movies, and refuses to enter into protracted discussions with Mae or anyone else. She pats the dog too hard on the head, and once in a while, she'll throw a screaming fit, jumping around beneath the pine trees, whooping and hollering for no obvious reason. She has small blue eyes with thick dark lashes, and two of her front teeth are crooked. Mae wants her to get braces, but Nola refuses. She also refuses to shave her legs, which have become quite hairy lately.

They are so different, mother and daughter, that I often find myself wondering about Nola's late father. Henry Tusk was a bio-chemist from Harvard who spent his time discovering by slow degrees how a virus attaches itself to a human cell. He was killed in a plane crash when Nola was eight. He was on the road, Mae believes, to finding a cure for cancer. Before he died, they worked in neighboring buildings and met for cappucino at umbrellaed cafes in Harvard Square.

I follow Nola down to the lake. Sun pours over everything; it's a beautiful day. She leaves her flip-flops on the shore, two melted footprints, and marches straight into the water without pausing, a toy soldier full of mechanical determination.

I watch from shore as she strides into the water, tadpoles stirring in her wake. Suddenly, she lands with a splash, her bottom going up, a flash of half-moons. More splashing, and then she disappears.

"Nola!" I cry, feeling immediately foolish. She must know how to dive, surely Mae has taught her how to dive. Her feet surface where feet shouldn't be—upside down and uselessly kicking. I race in after her. She's not very far out, but she's completely underwater, her face a pale mask under blue glass.

I scoop her up and carry her back to shore, pat her as she sputters and gasps. She looks at me, her face stripped of its haughty indifference and alive with fear—there in the crooked lips, there above the eyes—the contagious fear of a little girl who's been swallowed by water. I sit with her on the sand and let her sob against my shoulder.

"Daddy's dead!" she cries.

I try to soothe her as best I can. "You must miss him very much."

"You're not my daddy!" She pounds my shoulder, water droplets flying from her fists. "You'll never be my daddy. Never!"

"No," I say. "Not really."

"Then why are you adopting me?"

I shiver all over, take a deep breath, tell her the truth. "Because it's what your mother wants. She thinks it'll be good this way. We'll be a family."

"But you already have a family, Sam," she says, smacking me on the shoulder again.

Sam! She called me Sam! There is fury in the dark bend of her brow, fury and frustration. I can't help myself, I take her in my arms and hug her, squeeze her hard until she squeals. There's so much love here, I don't know what to do with it. "Now I'll have two families," I tell her. "Nola, I love you very much." My words, by comparison, sound soggy.

She looks me square in the eye without blinking, tears and lake water clinging to her cheeks. God, I love her steadiness, her intelligence, her unwavering honesty. "I know you do," she admits. She has broken her vow of silence; there is no turning back for us.

I stand, knees shaking. She fills me with such sadness and such pride.

On the way back up the hill, she runs ahead, her hair glistening pink in the fading light. She will run into her mother's arms. And later, I will tell Mae, "Your daughter spoke to me today." Already the words are forming inside my mouth. "She called me Sam," I'll say.

The Stuntman's Daughter

My stepfather Ty wants to play; he grabs me around the middle, knocks me to the floor, and I bite him hard on the arm.

"Ouch!" he cries, and I think, good. Good.

Mama's on a shoot in Inglewood and we're all alone in the camper. He rolls me over so I'm lying flat on my back on the cold, dirty floor and yanks my T-shirt up over my head. When I start to cry, he says, "Don't. I'll stop." But he doesn't stop. He's a liar.

I'm standing in the middle of the camper in my underwear, and my stepfather stands behind me. "Try this shirt on," he says, handing me the one with the yellow pinstripes. I put it on, long sleeves swallowing my hands, shirttails burying my knees. "Now the tie." He flips the collar up and slides a fat rust-colored tie around my neck. He stands so close behind me, I can feel the bulges of his body, and his breath slaps my neck like a lazy hand.

He says, "This is how you fix a tie, Leona. Watch the mirror." I automatically watch, afraid he'll look, and our eyes will meet and something awful will happen. His skinny fingers fumble as he swears. He grabs the shirt cuffs and wraps the sleeves around me like a straightjacket, pulling them tight, tighter, until I'm hugging myself. I hate him, hate his hands on me.

"Don't tell your mother." He pulls me to the floor. "If you do, I'll say it's all your fault. And she'll believe me; I'll make her believe

11

me. Remember that."

Black hairs unfurl from his nose and he stinks of cigarettes and his hands are warm all over me. He shuts his eyes and his eyelids flutter—paper-white as frog bellies and so thin, I could poke my fingers through to the other side. The cabbagy smell of his breath, the way he whispers, "Remember."

Mama married Ty four years ago, the week I turned nine. My real father was a Hollywood stuntman who died in a stunt car crash when I was seven. Daddy taught me how to drive, sat me in his lap and pressed the pedals while I shifted gears and turned the steering wheel. When I grew up, he said, I'd be Hollywood's number one stuntwoman.

"Remember," Ty says, a kind of love-word, and my back jerks against the dirty camper rug. He holds my cotton underpants in his fist and beats the floor, and I shut my eyes, trying to remember exactly when these games got started. But now he's sobbing, and I'm too tired to wonder anymore.

Summer night, Mama's lying in the hammock strung between our camper and a palm tree. She drinks a Sombrero and gazes at the sky. A million stars are out. Ty holds her dirty feet in his hands and massages her sore arches while she tells us about her day, how she had to stand for five hours straight on a street corner in Inglewood. She's an extra in the movies, has a Union card and everything. "Have you ever stood five hours straight, Leona?"

"No, Mama." I need to talk; today I got my first period, blackish blood whirling in the toilet bowl, staining my panties. A cool breeze lifts off the ocean and drifts past our heads, plays with our hair. We live in Venice behind Juice Smith's house, just two blocks from the beach. Juice Smith is a producer. He and Ty are best friends, drinking buddies. When Ty lost his film distribution job, Juice told him he could park his camper here until he found a new one. That was a year and a half ago.

Ty does odd jobs for Juice now. I stay out of their way mostly.

I've read over half the books that Mama's bought and never finished. Sometimes, Ty takes me for rides on his motorcycle. I cling to him like a silverfish, and we fly down Santa Monica Boulevard and watch the palm trees whoosh past as we weave in and out of the steamy traffic. Sometimes, when Mama is gone, Ty lets me drive Juice's truck. I stretch my legs, ease my foot off the clutch, and we jerk and bounce to the corner liquor store, where Ty buys two six-packs and a gallon of Gallo burgundy. Him letting me drive is our little secret, he says.

"We're supposed to be part of this street crowd, and we're not supposed to notice Dirty Harry stalking this crazed psycho-killer," Mama says. "We can't look at the camera, no, no, never." She shakes her head. "And we're not supposed to stare at Dirty Harry. As if no one's ever seen him before!"

When Ty laughs, a pile of lines collects under each of his eyes. "I've gotta tell Juice you worked with Clint Eastwood."

Juice makes porno pictures in his basement. The actresses he hires hang out in his backyard and drink white wine from long-stemmed glasses. They stretch out topless on yellow lawn chairs and have high shivering laughs, the kind that draw your attention. If I make the mistake of sitting outdoors, they try to get friendly and ask me dumb questions, like what am I gonna be when I grow up? Mama warns me not to put them down. "They're just doing their job," she says. "We've all got jobs to do."

Ty's tiny dark eyes focus on Mama's feet. He's small, almost pretty. Sometimes it surprises me how small and pretty he is—fine-boned, with delicate wrists and square ears so slender I could cover them with mussel shells from the beach. His hair is the same ugly brown as mine and falls in pencil-shaving curls. Mama's hair is long and red. She's got perfect posture and freckles on her legs. The two of us look hardly anything alike.

Ty stands and stretches, his lifted T-shirt exposing fine dark hairs that run down his chest toward his navel. "I'm going to the corner for some beer. Want anything, girls?" I hate it when he calls us 'girls.'"

After he's gone, I take his place and push the hammock back and forth. "Mama, I got my period, finally."

"Oh, you poor thing." She sips her Sombrero. "Hand me my purse." She gives me some aspirin, then gazes out at the horizon where the sun is setting. Her eyes glow orange, and her red hair shines like fever.

She's been in nine movies so far, only for a few seconds each. But in the last picture with Jack Nicholson, she was onscreen a full five minutes. She sits at a restaurant table behind him, and you can see her profile and her perfectly straight back beneath the tight red dress. The makeup man has put her hair up, and her white neck shows, her high cheekbones, the long line of her jaw. She could be a movie star.

"Mama." I grip the rope. "I don't want to live here anymore. Can't we move?" She acts as if she hasn't heard, just keeps on staring at the sky. My throat closes, and I stop rocking. "Mama? I hate living here with him."

"Him, who?"

"Ty."

She puts her hand over mine, her fingers ice-cold from the glass. "Don't talk that way, Leona. I know he's not your real father, but he cares so much about us. We're his only family."

And suddenly, I want to push her off the hammock and watch her fall. She'd land flat on her face in the grass.

"But I can't stand the way he looks at me."

Her eyes search the far corners of my face. My mouth dries shut. "Remember," I hear Ty say, and wonder who she'd believe, him or me?

"What d'you mean, Leona? Who looks at you?"

"Juice," I say softly.

"Juice?" She laughs. "Nobody's looking at you, sweetheart. Don't be silly."

Sometimes when Ty gets drunk, he and Mama fight, and he calls her names and makes her cry. Then he gets down on his hands and knees and begs her forgiveness. When Mama's gone, he gets drunk and never raises his voice above a whisper. He calls me his precious baby, his honeypie. He lets me smoke his mentholated cigarettes and laughs whenever I choke on blue ribbons of smoke. Once he rented a boat and took me sailing, showed me how to work the tiller and ease the boat through the high, rocky rollings.

"Can't we go someplace else, Mama?"

"We'll stay here until Ty finds a job."

"That could take forever."

She looks out over the sea and taps her ringed fingers on the side of her glass. "He'll find a job soon. He's got a few leads." Then she turns to me. "I love him, Leona. You don't understand that kind of love." But I want to understand. "Whenever I get mad, really fed up, he does something wonderful, like buying me flowers or saying he's sorry. Or else he'll go like this." And she smooths the hair straight back from my forehead. It feels like I'm dreaming.

Mama wakes me up the morning of my fourteenth birthday, her breath still boozy from her night out with Ty. She leans over the bed and says we'll have a real house soon; she's been saving up.

"What about Ty?"

"What about him, silly?"

I open my presents on the floor—four books, a blouse, a watercolor set and sketchpad. Then she puts on a broadbrim hat, kisses me goodbye, and heads out for a film shoot in the Mojave Desert.

That afternoon, it starts to rain. Rain comes down hard on the camper roof. Ty sprawls on his and Mama's bed with a bottle of burgundy and a jelly glass and keeps on pouring. His lips grow purple from the wine. He watches me as I read one of my birthday books.

"Your mother told me you got your period. Guess that makes you a woman now?" He seems excited, dark eyebrows spreading wide apart.

"Guess," I say, shrugging. I hate Mama; she tells him everything.

"Maybe you should go to a clinic?" He lights a cigarette, smoke uncoiling from a corner of his mouth. "Maybe you should get some protection?"

I don't answer; I don't even want to think about it. I hold the book closer to my face.

"Aren't you finished reading yet?"

"Nope," I lie. I haven't read one line, not a single word, not with him looking at me that way. His fingers keep sliding down the glass like watery white slugs. He licks his purple lips with the tip of his purple tongue, and smoke fills the room. The camper is very narrow and very long, painted pink. "Last of the hot pink campers," Ty calls it, joking. At night, I sleep at the opposite end on a foam rubber mattress behind one of those fake Oriental screens that Mama got from one of her movies. They were throwing it away because the panels were torn, but Mama glued the pieces back together.

"Becky's in the desert right now," Ty says, as if I didn't know it. "She's probably dying of the heat, and here we sit, nice and cool. Listen to that rain coming down, Leona. It never rains in California, it pours . . . ."

He puts his wineglass down, stands and starts undressing right in front of me. He walks around naked in his red socks. He gets a glass of water from the aluminum sink, and I hold the book closer to my face, words blurring together. Damp, hot, naked, drunk, Ty stands beside the sink. He is breathing heavy clouds of smoke behind my back.

"Leona," he whispers, but I don't answer. "Leona," he says in a voice I want to bury.

"Cut it out." My heart is pounding; I want to escape, but where would I go? Once I ran away to Juice's house, but I could see naked men and women rolling around on his living room floor through one of the back windows, bright lights and cameras pointed at them.

"Leona." I cover my face with my hands and listen to that awful voice, the pitiful pleading sound. I picture his penis, blind-hard, and his fingers sliding wetly down the aluminum sink. His skin's a white wall I can't climb; his voice is out to get me. "Leona . . . ."

Slowly, I lower the book. He moves around in front of me, and I hit him, beat his chest, his stomach, slap his hands away; but he grabs my wrists, holds me tight. "I want you to touch me nice," he says, twisting my arms. "Touch me nice!"

My hands shake as I stroke him. I stroke until his eyes roll up in their sockets. My hands work his slippery flesh until he groans, moans low like a cow, hisses in wonder. The come shoots thick and hot into my palm, and I cup my hands in my lap while he bends to lick tears from my eyes.

✻

On Mama's day off, Ty drives Juice's truck into town to run a bunch of errands. He'll be gone all afternoon. "Just us girls," Mama says.

We decide to have a picnic on the beach. She snaps open a beach towel, blazing white in the sun. A strong breeze blows, sprinkling sand over our food. My teeth crunch grits of sand as I bite into my sandwich. Today, I'm going to tell her everything.

"You ought to join a drama club," she says cheerfully. "You'd make a terrific actress. I wish I'd taken lessons when I was in school. I was watching Sally yesterday, and she's so brilliant. Maybe if I'd studied acting, I'd be as good as her? What d'you think?"

She plucks a pickle from the pickle jar, slides it over her tongue. She licks all the juice off before biting into it. "It was roasting in the desert. Everybody kept running into their trailers to cool off. We sucked ice all day. This one cameraman wrapped a towel around his head like an Arabian. A couple of people even fainted!"

"Mama," I say, "Ty touches me sometimes."

She looks at me as if I've let her down, drops the pickle in the sand. The wind picks up our hair, long black and red whips flicking across our faces. The ocean roars in my ears, making me dizzy.

"I don't know what you mean," she says.

"I mean he touches me sometimes."

"How? How does he touch you?"

Suddenly ashamed, I hang my head and want to cry.

She grabs me by the shoulders. "Leona, look at me. How does he touch you?"

"Ouch, Mama."

She shakes me hard. "Leona, look at me!"

Remember.

I look at her and almost faint. I'll be the best actress in the world, better than Meryl Streep. "He touches me here," I tell her, patting my arm. "And here." My hand.

"What on earth do you mean?"

"When he talks to me sometimes, he touches my arm like this, and I don't like it."

"Oh, darling, he's only being affectionate." She lets me go, relief filling her face like a sail catching the wind.

"But I don't like it."

"You're too self-conscious." She picks up the sand-covered pickle and starts dusting it off with her fingers. "You've always been self-conscious, even as a little girl." She dusts the pickle off and, once she's wiped it perfectly clean, tosses it back in the sand.

✳

Juice and Ty are out back playing cards and drinking, listening to the radio. Juice has bleach-blonde hair and a bad case of sunburn. He sits shirtless in his designer jeans at the umbrellaed table. Ty hates the sun. He wears a black fedora and the darkest Foster Grants, a tangerine, long-sleeve shirt. He wears pants even on the hottest days.

I'm sitting in the camper trying to read, but they keep boosting the volume. Now they're singing to an old Beatles' song, "Strawberry Fields Forever." I go outside and ask them to turn it down.

"Hey," Juice says, lowering the volume. "What's that you're reading?"

"Just a book."

"Lemme see." He grabs my book away, holds it about an inch from his face. "*The Life of James Dean,*" he reads so slowly, I can hardly believe he went to school. They've been drinking gin and tonics, and their eyes are bloodshot. He holds the book high over his head and laughs.

"Give it back," I say.

Ty snorts. "Leona's a woman now, didja know?"

"A woman, huh?" Juice looks at me as if we've never met, then snaps the book shut like a fat castanet. His dark blonde underarm hair smells of Old Spice. "A real woman, huh?"

"Shut up!" I try to grab the book away, but Juice holds it out of reach.

"She's got her period and everything."

I swing around and knock the cards out of Ty's hands. "Shut up!" A full house goes fluttering over the lawn. "I hate you!" He spreads his hands over the warped metal table and stares at his knuckles, snowy white in the sun.

"Want your book, Leona?" Juice says. "Come an' get it, come on . . . ." Each time I make a grab, he tucks it behind his back or over his head. "Jump, Leona, jump!"

"Leave her alone," Ty grumbles, reshuffling the deck.

"Jump, Leona!"

As I jump, he lifts my T-shirt and snaps the elastic band of my bra. "Hoooo-ee! She's a real woman, all right!"

I grab the book and run.

"Leona! Hey, don't be sore! I was only kiddin'."

I can hear their drunken laughter as I slam the camper door. I throw the book on the floor, dive into Mama's bed and bury my face in her pillow. I want to cry, but I can't. Instead, I laugh. I laugh so hard, I almost choke. I am coughing, sputtering, laughing.

I lie in Mama's bed awhile, inhaling her sweet scent, but Ty is also here—his spicy smell, curly-rooted black hairs clinging to the white sheets. I clutch my stomach, fold up like an embryo, and lie as still as the camper air. I want the ground to open up and swallow everything I know—the pier and all the palm trees and boulevards, even the cemetery where my father is buried.

Then a new feeling comes over me. My legs tremble and my scalp prickles as the blood rushes to my face. I can't stay here anymore. I fetch the keys to the camper and climb into the cabin. Holding the steering wheel as if I've held it all my life, I turn on the ignition.

Ty and Juice are hunched over their playing cards. They've forgotten all about me. Ty takes a long drink, his shaded face slick with sweat. As soon as I rev the engine, he looks up, alarmed. "Hey!" he says, dropping the glass.

I step on the gas pedal and the camper lurches forward, door handle popping as the hammock slaps back against the palm tree. I head straight for them—two men sitting at a round table underneath a blue-and-green cafe umbrella. I aim for Ty's white face, Juice's glistening back, and they leap from their chairs, running in opposite directions. As I hit the table, chairs explode and colors flash. The rear tires bounce, and I slam forward, busting my lip on the steering wheel. I can taste the blood in my mouth as I roll past lawn chairs and beach balls, striped towels and tubes of suntan oil. Through the rearview mirror, I see them stumbling after me—Ty so feeble and small, his face a vicious dot in the bright landscape.

The steering wheel shakes in my hands. Everything in back scatters as the camper jerks and veers. It's harder to handle than Juice's truck. Books fly off their shelves and knock into cabinet doors as I take a sharp left onto the road that leads to the highway.

I follow the Coast Highway north up the beach, past palm trees and bungalows, parked cars and cafes. Wind beats like drying sheets into the cabin, and the ocean air whips my face, numbs my lips. My eyes fill with tears from the stinging wind.

Wind whirls all around me, cold and salt-smelling. Sea gulls like paper kites catch a high breeze. As soon as I find a turnoff, I pull over and come to a jerky stop on the sandy, sloping shoulder. An old pack of playing cards flies off the dashboard, scatters over my lap and onto the floor.

I fumble in my jeans' pocket for my birthday money and count out twenty-five dollars on the seat behind me. "Okay," I say, and pull out again. I pass billboards and low-lying buildings, bars with blue neon signs. Mama is around here someplace, standing in a crowd, or else sitting at a table, her head held perfectly erect.

The camper needs gas. Beyond a cement guard rail, the ocean rocks restlessly. Suddenly cold, I roll my window up.

Annabelle

The windows in the surgeon's office are hermetically sealed. His desktop holds a framed picture of his wife, a coiled stethoscope, a vase of baby's breath, a handful of sharpened pencils, and Annabelle's file. Whenever Dr. Granger shifts in his chair, the chocolate leather squeaks.

Wally Morrison sits beside his wife, Rebecca, in an equally uncomfortable chair. He is tempted to reach for her. Her brow is pinched with worry, and she bites her fingernails one at a time.

Three-year-old Annabelle is in the next room with the nurse. Wally can see her through the cracked-open door. She squats over a plastic firetruck, her pale blue johnny slipping off one shoulder, her exposed spine a row of fisted knuckles. She has Rebecca's build— same stubborn barrel chest and slender legs—but her white-blonde hair resembles Wally's at that age. In old family photographs, his head is a bright flash, like a nick in the emulsion.

Dr. Granger wants to remove the excess tissue from Annabelle's mouth and tongue. He wants to reshape her eyelids so they won't have that distinctive "Mongoloid" look and pin back her ears. He draws careful diagrams and points at charts with the tip of a pencil. Moments ago, he touched Annabelle's face with gentle, disciplined fingers. Wally trusts him implicitly.

"After the operation, people won't be able to peg her," Dr. Granger now reassures them. "She won't be judged, stigmatized."

"But will it hurt?" Rebecca wants to know, balling up a Kleenex in her fist until it is the size and shape of a prune.

"She'll be under general anesthesia."

"But what about afterward?"

"Tylenol can be quite effective."

Down in the lobby, plugging quarters into the candy machine, Rebecca says, "This whole business is killing me."

✳

Sometimes late at night, Wally dreams that Annabelle's hands are exploring his face, her small body beside him on the pillow. He wakes in a panic, groping for her, but she is no longer there. He writhes in a tangle of damp sheets and bad breath, heart thudding in his chest, afraid to get up, afraid she might really be gone.

Once he has composed himself, he sneaks into her moonlit room and stands motionless at the foot of her bed, inhaling the sweet scent of baby powder and clean fitted sheets. Her breathing sounds like the beating of minuscule wings.

And later, he will dream that she is lost to him forever, hovering like a hummingbird above his bed, calling out their names.

✳

Rebecca kneels on the living room rug, swatches of cloth and papier-mache materials and scissors and paints fanned out around her. Her long braid hangs down her back like a second set of vertebrae. She is concentrating hard, pink tongue poking out as she outlines a dozen masks for Annabelle's preschool graduation ceremony.

Wally is chasing naked Annabelle around the house. She has an endearing, scrunched-up face with heavy-lidded brown eyes and ears like thumbs pointing east and west. She squeals delightedly each time he draws near, scoots behind the sofa, the television set, his easel. Wally and Rebecca are painters, but have other jobs for money. Wally does freelance computer work, Rebecca models for artists.

"Daddy, catch me!" Annabelle cries, then darts into the kitchen, bare feet padding across the linoleum floor. He scoops her up in his arms, her shrieks as piercing as knife pricks.

"Enough!" Rebecca hollers from the living room. Her legs are crossed Indian-style, and she scowls at him. They've been fighting all week about the operation.

"Okay, bath time, Anna-belly button." Cradling his daughter in his arms, Wally makes like a monster and blows a fart on her round belly.

"Again!" She scissor-kicks her legs.

All around them, other parents are raising superbabies. They crawl, walk, talk, and go to the potty earlier than the books predict they will. They say their first words, and their vocabularies blossom.

With Annabelle it was different. First, there was a long silence, longer than most. Then one word finally emerged, "Dada." Another, "Bup-ba." Another . . . .

Wally is careful to draw a tepid bath. Annabelle squinches her face on contact with the soapy washcloth. Before she was born, he never noticed retarded people. Now he spots them all the time—whole groups on community outings. They drool and gape, make inappropriate noises and gestures. And once a man in plaid highwaters and a lime-green windbreaker grabbed his arm and wouldn't let go. "Be my friend?" he kept saying, while the attendants pried them apart. That day, Wally decided his daughter would never lack for decent clothing—pretty dresses, matching outfits. No neon-pink coats or striped bellbottoms, ever.

Before he can finish tonight's bedtime story, Annabelle drifts off to sleep. Wally turns out the light and joins his wife in the living room. Rebecca dons one of the papier-mache masks. Flesh-colored and bumpy, it is like a coating of tumorous skin.

"What d'you think?"

"I think you should paint it blue or something."

"It's going to be purple," she says, not taking it off.

Wally crouches beside her, picks up a feather and tickles the nape of her neck. Rebecca shivers, laughs, turns for a kiss—her lips protruding obscenely through the mouth hole.

"Take that thing off."

"No." She grabs him, wrestles him to the floor, kisses him fiercely.

Her eyes gaze eerily at him through the eyeholes, and Wally struggles to break free. "Hey!" He pushes her away.

"I didn't think you'd like it," she says, hurling the mask at the wall, where it bounces and glides like a frisbee to the floor.

✳

"Ready?" Wally asks, taking Annabelle's hand. Over her jumpsuit, she wears a jacket the color of her favorite food, oranges. She's shorter than most children her age, smaller-boned. She can't run as fast or jump as high but is full of curiosity. She picks fat bouquets of dandelions, saves loose safety pins and her mother's used Kleenex in a shoebox hidden under her bed, chases pigeons down the sidewalk and speaks enthusiastically to strangers.

Wally used to play basketball with his buddies, but now he takes Annabelle on long walks through the neighborhood instead. Rebecca, who hates any form of exercise, never joins them. As soon as they are gone, he knows she'll devour the last can of tuna or half a jar of pistachio nuts. She'll help herself to the granola, tilting the bowl to finish off the bluish milk. She has gained thirty pounds in the three years since Annabelle was born, and her popularity as an artist's model has soared. "When you're fat," she tells him flatly, "there's more of you to draw."

Rebecca never lets him draw her nude. "I'm an artist, same as you," she snaps. He is jealous of the men he imagines sketching her long legs, her full breasts. She bristles at the suggestion she find another job. "What do you want me to do, be a secretary?" He thinks her paintings are full of rage, all reds and purples, like the pulsing insides of a womb or a heart.

The day is cool, a hint of wood smoke in the air. They live in a rent-controlled neighborhood, surrounded by brick sidewalks and brick condos. Wally lets Annabelle roam ahead; although she meanders, she is no less a handful. There are certain things she likes to do, like greeting the man at the corner grocery store. It has become a daily event, like her toothbrushing, shoe-counting, their walks together. Every morning, she places her juice cup in the exact same position on the woven place mat. She touches the faucet twice before turning on the water. The doctors have warned them about the highly ritualized behavior of Down's children. She becomes crabby if her routine is disrupted. She cries easily.

As an infant, she used to cry all the time. Wally and Rebecca hardly ever slept during those first few years. Even after the crying jags ebbed, Rebecca would toss and turn, heavy with worry. She developed the habit of worrying, and now she sometimes gets up in the middle of the night to work on a painting or sneak snacks from the refrigerator.

Now Annabelle is scampering toward a stranger, some derelict hanging around the laundromat. He wears an army jacket over a Marie Osmond T-shirt and khaki pants. Anxiety nags at the pit of Wally's stomach. The man's face is ruddy with sunburn and his greasy blonde hair drifts over his eyes.

"Annabelle!" Wally warns, but before he can stop her, she hurtles forward, arms outstretched, and the derelict lifts her off the ground. He twirls her around, her orange jacket bunching under her arms, her little legs flying out. Annabelle squeals with delight.

The air suddenly feels too thick to breathe. Wally charges after them, collides with them, hugging the man and Annabelle in an awkward embrace. "No, no!" he scolds, as if speaking to a very small child.

The lines carved into the man's leathery face seem to soften. His drunken eyes well.

"No," Wally says firmly, retrieving his daughter, clutching her tightly to his chest. He wonders if she can feel his thundering heart. He definitely won't mention this to Rebecca.

The man points at Wally's sneakers and says, "Nice hightops." His fingernails are caked with dirt so black it could be blood.

"I'm sorry." Wally backs away.

"Bye-bye!" Annabelle waves, straining at her father's grasp. "Bye!"

The derelict wiggles his dirty fingers at them.

※

"Want to fuck?" Rebecca asks. It is three in the morning. She has been fidgeting in bed beside him, keeping him awake.

Before he can answer, she says, "Oh, forget it. I don't really want to fuck."

Wally reaches for her, massages her neck, her soft, warm shoulders. "What's wrong, honey?"

"Forget it, I said."

Rebecca likes to sleep late on weekends, make love in the morning, and rinse her hair with lemons to bring out the auburn highlights. She sits in front of the television set, picking her fingernails, mouth slightly open, absorbed in whatever is on. They share studio space in Somerville, and the newspapers they spread over the floor become caked with dribbled paint, preserving their footprints—soles of Nikes, flips-flops, Rebecca's bare feet, ten toes, the littlest sometimes lost. She works in jogging pants and an old sweatshirt, while he wears shorts, red-and-blue-striped. He hops in the shower afterward, while she leaves streaks of raw umber and alizarin crimson on her elbows and fingers. In the morning she scrubs herself down with a kerosene-soaked rag before taking her daily bath. Making love to Rebecca is something like painting—same smells, same search for the right texture, all broad sweeps and attention to detail.

"You're still worried, aren't you?" he says now, directing long strands of hair away from her lips.

"Of course, I'm worried. Aren't you? I mean, have you absolutely no qualms? Christ, I didn't realize you were such a heartless prick."

"Whoa, time out." Wally gets up, paces the floor. "Listen, we've been over this a million times. It'd be better for her this way. It's hard enough being a 'normal' kid. They used to call me Wally Balls. Wally Cleaver."

"You told me." She picks up the alarm clock, starts fiddling with the dials. "And I wore braces and glasses, so what? What's that got to do with Annabelle having her face all carved up?"

"Rebecca, stop talking like that." She has kicked all the blankets and sheets down around her ankles. "Do you remember having your tonsils out? Can you remember being born?"

She slouches against her pillow, alarm clock resting in her lap. "All we do is talk about Annabelle. Annabelle this, Annabelle that. We don't lead normal lives anymore. We don't even fuck the way we used to."

"And will you stop saying 'fuck.' You make it sound so mechanical."

The day Annabelle was born, Wally expressed his shock and dismay to anyone who would listen, as if the doctors and nurses could somehow rectify their mistake. Rebecca, deep in an anesthetized stupor, didn't realize the gravity of the situation. In fact, it took her several days to acknowledge that anything was out of the ordinary.

Physically, Annabelle is perfect: ten fingers, ten toes, two arms, two legs, everything she needs for getting around the playground. Their pediatrician insisted that they treat her like an ordinary child. The greater their expectations, the more she will learn, grow. Blossom. Some children with Down's syndrome reach levels of unexpected intelligence, he tells them. It all depends. Hubert Humphrey had Down's; apparently the syndrome manifests itself in radically different ways. Their daughter will be retarded, but perhaps she can still lead an independent life.

"It'll give her the edge she needs," Wally says now, picking up the alarm clock. "I have to get up at six. Why'd you reset it?"

"But the pain . . . ."

"We're programmed to forget pain, Rebecca."

"I don't believe it. Oh, Wally, she's so young."

"Better now than later."

"How do you know?" She glares at him.

And he doesn't know. She's right; what does he know? But they need to make their decision soon, before Annabelle enters kindergarten and is able to remember other children's cruelty.

One thing he can't confess to Rebecca, the one thing that really bothers him, is how easily identifiable retarded people are. As if they had signs taped to their foreheads: "Kiss me, I'm retarded!" The biggest giveaway are the eyes—limp-lidded, slightly Asian.

Their ears stick out puppet-like, their faces are broad, their tongues protrude. There's an ephemeral quality about them as well, a kind of spaciness.

"I need some warm milk," Rebecca says, getting out of bed, and he knows she won't come back until dawn.

✳

"Where goin', daddy?" Annabelle tightens her grip. The three of them are crossing the park, where rows of golden tulips gape at them open-mouthed.

"Graduation, remember?"

"What's grah-dashun?" She watches him expectantly with her mud-colored eyes. It breaks Wally's heart how quickly facts slip from her memory. She struggles with her alphabet, drops things, sometimes forgets where she is and bumps her head.

"Graduation from preschool, butterfly."

"Where?" Her eyes light up.

"No, not 'butterfly,' sweetie," Wally says, laughing. He turns helplessly toward his wife.

Rebecca bends down to explain. "Preschool's over after today, honey. Next comes kindergarten. How about that, big girl?"

"Bee guh!"

"That's right." Rebecca hands Wally the salad bowl and bag of masks, and lifts Annabelle into her arms. "Suppose the surgeon makes a mistake?" she hisses at him over her shoulder. "Suppose one operation isn't enough?"

"Dr. Granger knows what he's doing."

"He may know what he's doing, but do we?"

Wally can't answer that. Squirming out of her mother's arms, Annabelle stands on the sidewalk between them. "Thwing!" she insists, noodling her knees so they have no choice but to lift her off the ground.

"Again!"

Rebecca's anger rivers away. "Little monkey." They never call her that in public, fearing strangers might think they're being cruel.

"Again!" Annabelle begs, hanging from their arms.

❋

Annabelle's preschool is located in the basement playroom of a large white colonial on Camden Street. A pair of sliding glass doors opens onto a backyard ringed with oaks and drowsing willows. The yard is equipped with a swing set, a jungle gym, and a bright red playhouse. Dozens of families have gathered around two picnic tables laden with PTA food—casseroles, hotdogs, chips and dip.

Wally shakes hands with Annabelle's teacher, Ginnie Kramer, a muscular brunette in a sky-blue Danskin, while Rebecca clears a space for her Waldorf salad. Then the two women disappear inside the house to discuss the masks.

Annabelle joins hands with her best friend, Kelly, who has long black hair and wide china-doll eyes. They dash away, leaving Wally alone. He grabs a beer and bumps into an art historian he's done some computer work for. Jerry Matz's T-shirt says, "Life sucks and then you die," with little happy faces replacing the dots over the "i's".

"Wally! I didn't know you had a kid here." Jerry is the kind of art historian who discovers symbols everywhere—hidden in a bowl of fruit, in the particular folds of a woman's dress. He still believes that Paul is dead.

"Over there." Wally catches the flash that is Annabelle and points her out.

Jerry's smile broadens, then freezes. "Oh, wow," he says, taking a moment to recover. "Cute! My nephew, Ben." He indicates the little hellion who's just knocked over a row of metal chairs set up in front of the makeshift stage across the lawn. "Excuse me," he says, hurrying away to play pickup sticks.

Rebecca rejoins him, holding a glass of white wine and a wedge of cheese. "She doesn't like them."

"Did she say so?"

"She didn't have to. I could see it in her face."

"What'd she say, Rebecca?"

She shrugs. "Great."

"See? That's just your insecurity talking."

"You weren't there when she opened the bag." Rebecca bites into the cheese and, looking at him oddly, says, "Faces speak words, y'know. Whole paragraphs."

Just then, a woman in a purple pantsuit approaches them with her hands clasped. Her clothes fit her loosely, as if they once belonged to somebody else. "Is Annabelle your daughter?" she asks. "I'm Avery's mom. We all adore her!"

Annabelle and Kelly are circling the monkey bars, where a group of wild-looking boys in white shirts, khaki shorts and little red bowties spin around the dull metal bars. Annabelle's rasping laughter tugs at Wally's heart. She isn't that different from all the rest. She can run, jump, catch a ball. He follows her lagging progress across the yard—her ruffling yellow dress, her blaze of hair—and feels a nagging tug in the pit of his stomach. He's so afraid she will fall. The other kids seem as careless as plummeting satellites. A boy, somersaulting too close, brushes Kelly's hair with his sneakertip . . . . but Kelly hardly notices.

Rebecca finishes her wine.

"You two must be so proud!" Avery's mom says.

"Oh, yes." Rebecca's smile is cold, brittle. "We plan on having three more just like her."

"Oh?" The woman blinks vacantly. "Excuse me, won't you?"

After she leaves, Rebecca refills her wine glass, and Wally can't help feeling a ferocious tenderness for her. "What're you doing?" he asks.

"I wanted to kick her." Her laughter is the kind that comes from deep inside, indistinguishable from grief. "Can you believe it? 'We must be proud.' What's she talking about?" Rebecca shudders. "That ingratiating smile."

"Calm down. She didn't mean anything."

"Didn't mean anything?"

"It's time!" Ginnie Kramer shouts, clapping her hands and herding twelve masked preschoolers up onto the plywood stage. As Wally takes his seat, his chair legs sink into the lawn, still soft from yesterday's rain. Annabelle scrambles onstage with Kelly and waves at them. "Hi, Mommy! Hi, Daddy!"

Kelly giggles.

Wally is mortified. The masks are grotesque. Twelve purple gremlins gape down at them. He wipes the perspiration from his upper lip. Ginnie Kramer switches on a tape recorder and starts swinging her arms to the beat. As she purses her lips together, a white circle forms around her mouth.

"Knock, knock, says the woodpecker!" The children's voices rise in squeaky harmony. "It's spring, wake up, knock, knock!"

They spin and prance and wave their arms. Annabelle does her best to keep up. Once the song is over, the children whip off their masks and wave at their families, who burst into applause at the sight of their faces.

"Thank you, children." Ginnie Kramer beams. Scallops of sweat decorate her Danskin. "Now it's time to tell our audience about our future plans. Who's first?"

Wally's back stiffens; he's afraid Annabelle will forget her lines, or else burst into tears. Rebecca seems to be shrinking from him, from the sun above their heads, her chair lower than his.

The art historian's nephew goes first, announcing in a raspy voice that he intends to be an astronaut and fly to Mars. Next comes a shiny-faced girl who wants to be a ballerina.

"And what about you, Annabelle?"

Wally catches his breath.

"A princess!" she lisps, swishing her yellow dress from side to side in a shy, flirtatious way. "A princess and a nurse . . . . so I can wear pretty clothes and help sick people!" Grinning, she plops back down in her seat.

Wally wants to race up to the stage and hug her. Squeeze her. Rebecca's warm body is shifting beside him. Her eyes well with tears. He can hear a chorus of "Awwws," followed by explosive applause.

The woman in the purple pantsuit stands to cheer. Jerry Matz turns and winks at Wally, who feels itchy all of a sudden. His clothes are too tight. His chair keeps sinking deeper into the lawn.

The applause goes on and on. Finally, Kelly stands to complete silence. "I'm going to be a nurse, too," she says shyly, then abruptly sits. The applause for her is scattered and indifferent, buoyed only by her family's cheers.

Rebecca spills some wine. "Oops," she says. "Yeah, Kelly!" she shouts. "Oh, shit," she hisses, wiping at the stain blossoming on her blouse. Behind them, somebody snickers.

The rest of the children want to be firemen, teachers, and nurses—there is a surplus of nurses—and one little boy wants to be a stockbroker.

Rebecca's plastic cup is at her feet. "I'm drunk," she whispers in Wally's ear.

"That's okay." He squeezes her hand, wishing he could absorb her pain so she won't ever cry again, or toss and turn in the middle of the night, or eat half a cheesecake all by herself.

"Thank you, children!" Ginnie Kramer leads the applause, then switches on the tape recorder once again. The children sing about tigers and lions lurking in the jungle. They roll their eyes, clap their hands, and suddenly Annabelle wanders too close to the edge of the stage and tumbles off.

There is a collective gasp. Ginnie Kramer, too busy disciplining a wayward boy, doesn't seem to notice. Wally springs from his chair. "Annabelle!"

She pitches headfirst onto the grass, her yellow dress flying up behind her. He swears he can hear the thud of impact above the din of discordant voices.

"Oh, God." In a flickering instant, all the horrors of his imagination come alive; he sees Annabelle bleeding, Annabelle in a wheelchair, Annabelle in a small, white coffin.

Fear pinches the soft folds of her face. She's on the verge of crying, and Wally is right there with her, teetering on the brink. He can read whole passages in her sweet face, an entire library.

But now she is bounding gamely to her feet, wiping the grass stains off her hands. She hurries over to him. "Daddy!"

"You okay, sweetie?" She leaps into his arms; and suddenly he is hugging them both—Rebecca and Annabelle—holding them just as tightly as he dares.

"Oh, God, I love her face!" Rebecca's breath is hot against his cheek.

"Me, too."

Behind them, distracted preschoolers struggle through the rest of the song. "Roarrrr-rr, says the lion! Watch out!"

Wally, lifting Annabelle high above his head, asks, "Who's my little monkey?"

And that night, he dreams about her face shining in the sun.

Blindfold

Carla had a strong, clear alto. I knew because I stood next to her on the chorus platform. That was how we got to know one another. I never would've approached her otherwise.

Facing Mr. Romanski, I got a good look at Carla's profile—the jutting chin, the slender nose with its sensitive nostrils, those spooky eyes the color of some exotic tropical fish. Phosphorescent blue. She had long straight hair and wore tie-dyed T-shirts, golf shoes and huge beaded earrings. She belonged to a small band of weirdos, a group that included her boyfriend, Duncan. Duncan was blind. He was tall and had white hair. The other kids used to poke fun at him—the way he'd swing his cane like a weapon as he walked down the halls, everyone leaping out of his way; the mirrored sunglasses he always wore—until Carla became his girlfriend. Then nobody so much as snickered when he took out a braille book or nodded his head to a beat nobody else could hear.

In chorus, Carla would try to crack me up by pinching my arm, or else snatching away my sheet music in the middle of a song. Then I'd have to try to get it back without creating a scene. All the while she'd be singing angelically, sending me these little half-smiles, her exotic eyes glinting with suppressed laughter.

She was all angles and surprises, like a cactus. Before chorus, she'd prop herself on the edge of the stage and watch the rest of us as we settled into our seats and shuffled our sheet music. She always managed to put her cigarette out moments before Mr. Romanski came barreling in, fanning the air with Irving Berlin's "God Bless America." He'd glare at us as if we were all guilty, then tap his baton on the music stand.

That was how it started. I'd been struggling with my insecurities. I kept outgrowing the clothes my mother never replaced fast enough. I hated my high-pitched, irritating laugh. I tried to be as cool as Harold Sherman, the senior who listened to jazz . . . . or else Arnie Barkowski, the star quarterback with his dumb but winning smile. I couldn't understand why Carla, who was so beautiful, would have anything to do with me. But then one day, she invited me to go with her and Duncan and a few others to this great place they'd found, and that was when the trouble started.

The park was located two towns over, opening off the manicured yards of a string of renovated saltboxes. "A bunch of fatcats live here," Carla explained. "Lawyers and businessmen, just your basic scum of the earth."

She was wearing an orange T-shirt with a yellow sun blazing from the center, her nipples showing through the fabric since she didn't believe in bras. Her black jeans had dime-sized holes in the knees, and her red-beaded earrings dripped from her earlobes like blood. She took Duncan's hand as we crossed the street to the park, which was actually a forest with paths and a few clearings with picnic tables. The air was heavy with the songs of birds, and sunlight rippled through openings in the canopy of leaves above our heads. As we walked along, Carla described it all to Duncan.

"How many birds?" he asked. "How tall is this tree? What's that smell?"

There were four of us altogether—me and Carla and Duncan and a girl named Sylvia. Sylvia had stringy black hair and black eyes and no sense of humor. She kept yawning at everything I said, as if I was a jerk or something, and tugging on her stringy black hair. She had this habit of pulling out the hairs growing over her left ear and leaving a little bald patch. She wore a purple batik minidress, and even though I didn't like her much, I thought her legs were sexy. They were long and creamy white, and with each step her calves tensed.

It was two in the afternoon. I'd skipped geometry to be with them and was feeling kind of guilty, but also flattered, since I was the only sophomore. The rest were juniors and seniors. I kept think-ing how disappointed my mother would be if she ever found out, but Carla had me convinced: "You won't learn everything from a book, Bo."

The park was pretty much deserted. Duncan folded his elasti-cized cane into four neat pieces and looped it through his belt. He held Carla's elbow, and every once in a while, just as he was about to walk into a bush or tree stump or something, she'd say, "Careful, babe." Babe, she called him. That made my heart pound.

"You ever get high?" Sylvia asked me.

I nodded, which was a lie. I had a friend who'd gotten high once, and he told me it was sort of like drinking beer, which I'd done. He said you just got drowsy and felt sort of horny, or else famished. He'd eaten an entire Sarah Lee carrot cake all by himself.

"I'll bet."

"I have so." My voice squeaked.

"Who'd you smoke with?"

"My buddy, Deke Shreider." Another lie. Deke would've thrown up at the suggestion.

Deke and I grew up three houses apart. When we were little, we used to have pissing contests in the frog pond behind my house. We traded baseball cards and Tonka trucks and ghost stories, and once I even dared him to touch the walloping turd he'd left in our basement toilet. Deke was always playing Robin to my Batman. I'd say things like, "To the Batmobile, Robin," and he'd say holy this, or holy that. Or else he'd imitate Curly, pretending to poke me in the eyes. "Nyuck-nyuck-nyuck!"

"Deke, the geek?"

"He's no geek." I reached out to flick her hair. "At least he's not going bald, like some people."

She ducked behind her hands and screamed.

"Shut up, you two," Carla snapped, and I felt my face flushing. I didn't want her thinking I was a jerk. I moved away from Sylvia and pretended to admire the flora and fauna.

We came upon a clearing, sunlight punching through the tangle of branches as if the day had decided to suddenly open up and re-

veal its true beauty. I ran around like a lunatic, picking up stones
and shooting them at squirrels.

"Stop it," Sylvia said, "you're scaring the birds away!"

I looked back. Duncan and Carla were locked in each others'
arms, rolling around on the grass, and Carla was kissing him, moving her head in a way that made my mouth hurt. I couldn't believe
how happy they were, like little kids. I'd never heard her giggle so
much. Duncan smoothed his hands around her waist as if he could
feel her bare skin through her clothes, and I wondered if that was
why she liked him so much. Because of his touch, made sensitive
from years of blindness?

Sylvia plopped down in the middle of the clearing and tilted
her face toward the sun. Then she crossed her legs, rested her hands
on her knees and started humming, and I laughed. The wind out-
lined her breasts and nudged at the hem of her dress, exposing her
thighs.

Carla took out a joint, lit it, then pushed the hair out of her face.
"Here, Bo."

I was really nervous and tried not to choke. We passed the joint
around, and as it got easier to inhale, I started noticing how the leaves
seemed to be falling in slow motion from the trees. I remember laughing with my mouth full of smoke. I got all caught up in the way
Carla shook her head when she laughed and the way her dark hair
rested against her shoulder, like a photographic negative of snow
blowing through an open door. I remembered my parents as they
were in a ten-year-old photograph, and then my eyes just fixed on
Sylvia's necklace, something I hadn't noticed before—this tiny gold
chain with a gold word at the base of her neck. *Aires,* gold lassoes
for letters, riding her pulse. My thoughts felt about thumbsized.

Sylvia got up and twirled around in the sunshine, and Duncan
and Carla were kissing again, and I kept thinking, if only I could
teach myself to touch without looking, then maybe I'd have a chance
with her?

The next day, Carla showed up on my doorstep. I answered the
door bare-chested, dirty jeans hanging low on my hips. "Oops," I
said, holding the door half-shut. "I thought you were Deke!"

"You gonna invite me in, Bo?" She craned her neck.

"I don't think so."

"Why not?"

"Not today." I didn't want to tell her it was because I was embarrassed; I hadn't explained about my weird family yet. My father owned a home furnishing outlet, and our house was fixed up like a showcase. He brought all his clients over to view his merchandise in "the proper setting." There was a piano in the living room nobody ever played, a marble fireplace, Oriental rugs, half a dozen Italian lamps cocked at different angles in the corner over by the French doors. There were price tags on everything. My mother kept the house spotless. Her idea of gardening was to order a bunch of potted plants for the sunken garden; she'd rearrange them while I filled in the gaps with dirt.

My sister and I weren't allowed to scuff the floors or leave stuff lying around, not even in our own rooms. The entire house was open for inspection. Large white cabinets lined my bedroom walls, hiding my comic book collection and all my junk. We rarely had friends over; it was too hard to explain. Better just to go over to other kids' houses. My sister spent most of her time lying on her huge walnut canopy bed, talking on the phone. That bed was like her life raft.

"What, I've got cooties or something?" Carla said now, her fingers clamped over the door jamb.

"No, nothing like that." I laughed.

"What then?"

"Today's not a good day, that's all . . . . maybe another time?"

"Promise?"

"Sure."

"Cross your heart and hope to die?"

"Why not?" I said, crossing my ribs, hoping like hell she wouldn't hold me to it.

The following Saturday at the park, Carla made Sylvia and me put on blindfolds. She'd brought some scarves that smelled of her perfume. I chose the turquoise one I'd seen her wear before, and Carla pulled it taut, making sure I couldn't cheat.

"Okay now, the four of us are blind," she said. "Only Duncan knows his way around. Remember, first one to take off his blindfold's a chickenshit."

"Jeez," I said, "this feels weird." Even with a little light leaking through, I felt disoriented. I forgot which way I'd been standing when she first wrapped her scarf around my head.

Just then, a hand jabbed my back. "Who's that?"

"Me. Watch where you're going." Sylvia jabbed me again, then started tickling my ribs.

"Wow, Bo! Is that your real laugh?" She mimicked me, sounding like Alvin the Chipmunk having a heart attack. "Hee-hee-hee!"

"Hey . . . . I can't help it!"

"That's the laugh he was born with," Duncan said soberly. "Man, you've got to accept what you're born with."

We stopped fooling around, suddenly reminded of what we were supposed to be doing there, experiencing Duncan's blindness. Then I tripped over a rock and fell flat on my face.

"I'm taking this thing off," Sylvia said. "I don't care if I am chickenshit."

"You've only had it on for a *second*." Carla could stop a person cold with just the sound of her voice. "Duncan's been blind his *whole entire life*."

"Oh, you're right. All right."

Duncan had a throaty laugh. "This is fun."

"I think I know the way out," Carla said.

I stopped wiping the grit off my face and said, "The way out? We're not walking all the way back like this, are we?"

"Why not?" Carla's tone demanded a good reason, but I couldn't think of one.

"What if somebody sees us? Won't they think we're weird or something?"

"So what? You can't go through life being afraid of what other people think, Bo."

"Look," said Duncan. "Take my hand. We'll form a chain."

"Where are you?" Sylvia sounded far away. "Hey, you guys? *Help!*"

I tore off my blindfold, sunlight smacking me like a wet gym towel. Sylvia was tangled in the underbrush over by the dogwood trees, still blindfolded. She kept tugging her dress away from the thickets which clung by their prickers to her clothes. I could see her underpants. They were pink. I couldn't believe it.

I glanced at Duncan, still groping for somebody's hand over by the picnic tables. Carla stood about a yard away, holding the scarf away from her eyes. She'd cheated, too. We were both chickenshits. I thought she was going to lecture me to cover up her embarrassment, but instead, she just smiled.

I took a trembling breath; we'd cheated together, Carla and me. And I realized at that very instant how much I loved her. My legs almost buckled. A mild breeze kicked up, lifting her hair and whisking it across her face. I could smell her wildflower perfume in the scarf around my neck.

"Hey!" Sylvia shrieked, tossing her blindfold to the ground. "Look at you two, just standing there! Won't somebody come over and help me, please?"

The following week, all the kids at school thought it was strange when the weirdos started eating lunch with the Special Ed class. Special Ed usually ate by themselves at a wobbly table in a corner of the cafeteria. There was a retarded girl named Candy, a Jewish deaf boy named Irving, a boy with cerebral palsy named Jimmy K., and Duncan. The weirdos consisted of Carla and Sylvia, two twins named Roger and Roland, who were trying to grow goatees, and Duncan. Duncan was the common denominator.

At first, the whole school was cracking jokes about the Freak Table. But after a while, they got used to it. Deke thought the weirdos only made the Special Ed kids look worse, but I explained what Duncan had told me. "You've got what you've got, man." I waved my hand dismissively. "You should be proud of who you are."

"You've been disagreeing with me a lot lately." Deke's face sagged, and I felt pretty bad, but I no longer wanted to play Batman to his Robin.

"I'm just seeing things more clearly, is all," I explained, trying to sound lighthearted about it.

Deke twisted his Oreo cookie apart, scraping the icing with his front teeth. Making a stack of the chocolate wafers, he crammed them into his mouth. Crunch, crunch. For the first time ever, I thought maybe he really was a geek.

When Carla invited me to sit with them at the Freak Table, I didn't say yes right away. It was one thing to cut classes for afternoon trips to the park, but another to expose myself to the entire school as one of the Weirdos who sat with the Spazzes at the Freak Table. I told her I'd think about it.

"Make your decision now, Bo," she said, watching me carefully. Her eyes were the strangest color I'd ever seen, like watercolors blended together by accident. "You've got to decide whether you're going to be one of the leaders in this school, or one of the sheep. There's a whole new world out there, buddy."

Buddy! I didn't want to be called buddy, I wanted to be her babe.

That night, I dreamt about sheep. I was standing in the middle of a dirty flock, getting smothered by their heavy woollen bodies. I could hear their hooves hitting the dirt and their pathetic bleating, and suddenly I realized we were being herded through a gate into this cramped little pen.

The next day, I sat at the Freak Table.

The Special Ed kids weren't as scary or bizarre as I'd imagined. Irving, the deaf guy, taught me how to sign. He could read lips as long as you spoke carefully enough. Jimmy K., the boy with cerebral palsy, was almost exactly my age—two days younger—and collected comic books. He was difficult to understand, so I kept our conversations short, but Carla assured me it got easier. It knocked me out that he owned over a hundred issues of Batman, all in mint condition; still, I wasn't ready to visit his house just yet.

Toward the end of the week, Carla had another brilliant idea. Since it was so beautiful out, she said, why not have our lunch in the softball field? Never mind that a bunch of punks hung around out there; never mind that girls with teased-up hair and long white nails smoked cigarettes in the shade of the bleachers. She wanted to go. We could all use the sun, she said.

Out on the softball field, Carla and Sylvia danced between the bases, shouting, "I'm a sea gull! I'm an eagle!" They wove daisies into Candy's curly red hair. Candy seemed just like any other girl until she opened her mouth. "I love you, Bo," she said. "I love you," she told Carla and Duncan. "I love you!" Irving waved her away in disgust.

"Isn't that great? See, Bo? She's onto something. She knows what it's all about," Duncan said, plucking several tough blades of grass from the hardened soil. Thwup, thwup, thwup. Sandwiching a fat one between his thumbs, he put it to his lips and blew, making a piercing whistle. The whistle got the attention of the greasers and greaserettes behind us. *Bleeeet!* The hairs on the back of my neck stood up.

Irving was busy showing Carla how to sign the lyrics to "Runaway Train," while Sylvia sat at the foot of Jimmy K.'s wheelchair and demonstrated the proper way to meditate. Jimmy K.'s head kept swinging around, his eyes rolling around in their sockets, and I wondered how he ever stayed focused.

Bleeeet!

Now I glanced behind us, my worst nightmares confirmed. A couple of tough-looking hoods were standing there, glowering at us. My stomach tensed, and I could feel the sun beating down on my scalp. "Carla," I whispered.

She was tucking a huge daisy behind Candy's ear.

"I love you," Candy said.

"Those guys over there look pretty pissed off. I mean, this is their turf, right?"

"Don't sweat it," she said. "I know those guys, they're the biggest wimps."

"Oh." I felt about this small. Of course Carla knew those guys; she knew everybody. Carla was tougher than most of the punks surrounding first base, cigarettes drooping from their pouty lips.

Bleeeet!

"Uh, Duncan . . . . I don't think you should be doing that."

"Why not?" *Bleeeet! Bleeeeet!*

One of the guys approached us. He was wearing a black leather jacket despite the heat. He grabbed Duncan by the shirt collar and hoisted him off the ground. Duncan was tall, but this guy was taller, and bigger around, thick as a two-car garage. He lifted Duncan so high in the air, his feet dragged over the grass. He tossed Duncan in the dirt, and when he landed, a cloud of dust rose up. He didn't say a word.

"Hey!" Carla screamed.

We ran over to where Duncan lay spread-eagled.

"Are you hurt, babe?" Carla asked, leaning close, and I realized with a sinking feeling that no matter how much I wanted her to, she was never going to call me babe.

Duncan groaned as she raised his mirrored glasses to his forehead, and for the first time, I saw his eyes. They moved back and forth without purpose, like caged animals. They were deep-socketed, the irises and pupils almost the same color—a milky blue.

"I'm okay, Carla," he said, groping for his cane. "No big deal. Who did it?"

We all glared at the back of the tall, leather-jacketed creep who'd just tossed our pal in the dirt like a bag of stale Cheese Puffs.

"Travis Gordon, the idiot!" Carla screamed. If he heard, he never let on. "Bigot! Sleazeball!"

I stood there wondering whether or not I should chase after him. It might put me in Carla's favor, I thought, but just then Irving, his face twisted with rage, took off. He hop-scotched around Travis like a mad flea, arms working the air over good.

Travis turned and glared, while Irving made the sign for "Asshole," running his finger around inside a circle he made with his left hand. He was calling Travis an asshole, only Travis didn't know it. Then, looking as if he were stirring a large pot of soup, Irving signed, "Big asshole! Big asshole!"

"Ungh," Travis Gordon grunted, shoving him aside.

Before school ended, one of the most popular girls in school, a cheerleader with long, strawberry-blonde hair, joined us at the Freak Table. One moment, she was head cheerleader and Junior Class Treasurer, the next she was weaving flowers through her braids. Most kids thought the change was due to the fact that her boyfriend, Arnie Barkowski, had started fooling around with her best friend. But when

Debbie joined us at the Freak Table, she explained she was sick of conforming.

I could tell right away that Debbie was after Duncan, but Carla didn't seem to notice. Every day at lunch, Debbie would squeeze in between Duncan and me at the table and laugh loudly at his jokes. She'd lean in close whenever he spoke, tips of her long blonde braids dipping into her soup. She touched his elbow whenever she asked him a question. Her strong perfume made my bologna sandwich taste metallic in my mouth.

The days grew long and warm. We drank beer and drove to the beach and out to the country, where the smell of pig manure mushroomed for miles. I'd take one, maybe two hits off the joint and gaze out at the lonely acres of corn and alfalfa, the dumb spotted cows grazing in the fields. Then I'd focus my attention on Carla's laugh, or else the way her eyes crinkled when she smiled.

One day, while we were driving around, Carla announced that we were going to visit Bo's house. At first, I just laughed. She couldn't be serious. Then I panicked.

"Great," Sylvia said. "Bo's house."

"What fun!" Everything was a real kick to Debbie.

I tried to think of an excuse while Roland swung the van around. We zipped past telephone poles and mailboxes and American flags and dilapidated barns and gas stations with rusting pumps. I didn't want them to see all those price tags everywhere. My bedroom cabinets had been lacquered and varnished until their surfaces shone like polished stone. Sometimes my father would smooth his hands across the veneer. "How do you like them apples?" All he talked about was carpet napping and ceiling texture and how many different kinds of wood paneling there were, the perfect placement for a pair of matching Queen Anne chairs. Once he stayed up half the night rearranging the folds on a pair of satin drapes, fussing with the way they fell to the floor.

When we were little, my sister and I would disappear down to the basement playroom where our scattered toys didn't bother anyone. We'd pretend some old blanket was a tent. Lying side by side on the floor, eating marshmallows out of the bag, we'd imagine we were living in the wilderness or on Mars or something.

All the old demo models ended up in the basement. I'd lie on the camelback couch and read, or else listen to music and dream about Carla, a Tarreyton wedged between her fingers, and pretend that she loved me.

"Up this hill," she now said.

Carla led the way. I unlocked the door, thinking that, with any luck, we'd be in and out in no time. "I want you guys to know," I said, gripping the doorknob, "that none of this stuff . . . . that my father is, like . . . ."

"Oh come on, Bo," Carla said, brushing past me.

The front hall opened onto a high-ceilinged living room with gilt-framed mirrors, gaudy vitrines and a multitude of table and floor lamps. The sofa's slipcovers glistened in the sun. Everybody piled up in the doorway.

"See, my dad . . . ." I said, but just then, Carla clasped my hand.

"You poor thing!" Her eyes filled with tears. "No wonder you didn't want to let us in!" Then she burst out laughing.

Sylvia and the twins went over to the sunken garden and started picking flowers. Candy bounced on the couch, whomping the pillows with her feet. Debbie twirled in a pool of sunlight, while Duncan tapped his way through the maze of angled lamps in the corner. He made a false turn and knocked one of my father's prized Calvettis over, its lightbulb shattering.

There was silence. Debbie gaped in horror, but Carla only squeezed my hand. "Finishing touch!" she said, giving me a quick kiss that lingered like a sting.

That night, my parents sat me down and asked what the hell had happened.

"I had some friends over," I said.

"Is everything all right, Bo?" asked my mother, her lips pinched with worry.

"Couldn't be better."

My father tugged at his shirt collar. He had a ring of slate-colored hair that puffed out behind his ears. "I'd like to know what happened to my Calvetti." I could feel his hot breath on my cheek.

"That's an expensive lamp."

"One of my friends, who happens to be blind, knocked it over by accident."

My father drew back, startled. "You've got a friend who's blind?"

"Yeah, I've got blind friends."

"Since when?"

"Look, it was an accident, okay? That doesn't mean I'm not going to invite them over again. This is my house, too. Next time though, I'll take them down to the playroom, how's that?" I excused myself, feeling better than I had in ages, as if all my finals had been cancelled.

My elation didn't last long. By suppertime, I was apologizing, offering to pay for the lamp out of my allowance or something.

But my father surprised me. He told me to forget it.

During the last week of school, Duncan broke up with Carla and started dating Debbie. The whole school was buzzing with the news.

Carla acted as if she'd been hit by a truck. She came to me for comfort.

"She told him we were kissing, Bo! Isn't that the stupidest thing you've ever heard?"

"Not really."

"I give you a peck on the cheek, and she convinces Duncan we're going together or something. Conniving slut."

We headed for the park where we could talk things over. Carla drove her father's Oldsmobile Cutlass, and we rolled down the windows so our hair blew straight off our foreheads. Every couple of miles, she lit another cigarette off the butt of the last.

"I don't hate her," she said. "I don't hate anybody, Bo. I just want Duncan back. Listen, I'm going to ask you a big favor. You don't have to do it if you don't want, but could you . . . . not spy on them, exactly . . . . talk to Duncan man-to-man? Find out what's so special about her?"

"What good'd that do?"

"It can't last," she insisted. "Debbie's only going out with him because he's blind. Because it's 'fashionable' at the moment, you know? I made it the thing to do. She's imitating me. That's what's so irritating. I'm in love with Duncan, but she's just this little camp follower. Why doesn't she go back to Arnie and leave Duncan alone?"

I took one of her slender cigarettes out of the pack and placed it between my lips. I didn't inhale, just let the smoke sit there on my tongue.

"Listen," she said, "you don't know about Duncan. He breaks my heart." Her eyes were shiny. "One of his biggest dreams is to drive a car someday. He just wants to see how it feels."

The smoke came out of my mouth in a great puff.

The clearing must have brought back memories, because all of a sudden Carla burst into tears. Just like that, I was holding her. She sighed against my neck. I could feel her heartbeat through our clothes, and my T-shirt was soaked where her wet face rested. She tilted her head, and I kissed her. She tasted of salt and tobacco, grit from the road.

We lay down on the grass and held each other lightly. I wanted to kiss her again, but she seemed content to just lie there beside me. Bugs hopped over our bare arms, and birds flitted through the sky above our heads.

"Do you want to kiss me again, Bo? Am I pretty?"

"Yes."

"I'm glad." Her eyes were slanted shut, and I drew a little closer but she pushed me away. "I don't think it's a good idea, though."

"So how come you let me?"

"Not everyone can be strong all the time."

"I know," I said, but I didn't believe it. Batman could be counted on, and Robin was at least consistent.

Lying there in the hot afternoon sun, I started to think about my sister. Carla reminded me of her, of how lonely she was. Sometimes, late at night, when she got scared of lying all alone in her big, pink canopy bed, she'd sneak into my room and I'd make room for her head on my pillow. We'd tell each other ghost stories, or else we'd remember the past, how we used to visit our grandparents in Maine before they passed away.

"Look," Carla said, getting up and stretching, "you've been a big help, Bo. You're a true friend. But I think we'd better go."

"Okay," I said, brushing the grass stains off my jeans.

All during the summer that followed, Deke and I raced our dirt bikes up and down Reservoir Road. We rode to the gravel pits, or else took the motorcycle trail that stretched beneath the power lines connecting our town to the rest of the county. We passed the park but never went inside. Deke didn't ask me what'd happened there. I always felt saddest when he said things like, "Holy Kawasaki, Batman!"

Next summer, I knew, I wouldn't be doing this anymore. I'd already asked my father about getting a '68 candy-apple red Mustang I'd seen in Bernie Crispell's Oldies But Goodies. Who knew? Maybe I'd take Duncan to Grogin's Field, where we could drive around in circles without hitting a thing. And as soon as he picked up enough speed, I'd show him how to shift gears.

The Boarder

His name was Jack Knowledge. We giggled when we heard that. He was tall and thin and drew his hair into a ponytail, wore T-shirts and jeans and a big black cape, just like Dracula. He was five years younger than Mama and taught English at the community college where our father used to teach ceramics. He was the only one to answer Mama's ad for a boarder.

She put him up in the small attic room where Grampa used to stay. My sisters and I helped her scrub the floors and dust the ceiling and wash the only window, the one that overlooked the dangerous curve on Ruby Road. We pushed the bed away from the wall, dead flies crunching under our feet like peanut shells, and dusted the window fan's blades through the wire grill.

At first, we hardly ever saw the boarder. He woke up early, used the bathroom for half an hour, then drove off in his mustard-colored Mustang and didn't come back until dark. After a few days, Mama stopped setting an extra place at the breakfast table, which was fine by me; I hated seeing a plate, knife and fork where our father used to sit.

All that winter, I had nightmares about Dad. Sometimes I dreamt I was running through a maze, trying to escape before the world ran out of oxygen. But there was no way out, not even when I lifted off the ground and began to fly. Then I'd be running for the school bus without any underpants on. I'd wake up shaking just as the bus driver opened the door.

Other times, I dreamt Dad was talking to me in a very ordinary voice, asking me why I hadn't done better on a math test. I dreamt about him swimming in the neighbors' pool, and sometimes he'd get his foot caught in the drain, and I'd be the only one who could save him. Except I never saved him in my dreams, and he never managed to save me.

When Jack Knowledge's schedule changed that spring, Mama set an extra place at the table again. He got up later than usual, hogging the bathroom while the four of us waited impatiently for him to be done. He left huge piles of T-shirts and jeans and gray underpants all over the attic floor. We knew, because whenever we went up there to play with our train set, we'd see them—piles and piles of dirty clothes, left where they'd fallen.

One day, Mama collected all his dirty clothes and took them to the laundromat. I went with her. She pumped quarters into the machines. Her face grew red and hot as she carted the damp, heavy clothing from one machine to another, flicking out shirts, folding pants, balling up socks. When she was done, we hauled the piles back out to the car and carried them up the attic stairs, where we left them on Jack Knowledge's bed. "Won't he be surprised!" Mama said.

That night, when he came home, Mama told us not to say a word. Paige and Jo and I sat in front of the TV set, giggling and shushing one another, listening for his footsteps on the attic stairs. He usually changed clothes first thing when he got home, then ran water in the bathroom for about twenty minutes. Mama never got mad at him for wasting water the way she did with us.

He came downstairs in a clean shirt and jeans with creases in the legs. He kept brushing the hair off his face, trying to make a ponytail, but the elastic band snapped, and his long hair clung to his head like a girl's. "Did you do this?" he asked Mama, pointing at his shirt.

Her face was round and smiling. "Me and Mimi," she admitted.

"I'd rather you'd asked me first."

She got up from her desk and disappeared into the kitchen, saying, "Sorry," her voice trailing off. "Dinner's almost ready."

We sat frozen in our seats in front of the TV set while he followed her into the pantry. We could hear them very clearly.

"It's not that I don't appreciate the thought, Beth," he said, "it's just that I don't want you going to all that trouble."

"It wasn't any trouble."

"Believe me, I know it must've been."

"No, really. I had the girls' wash to do."

"What a lie!" I hissed. Jo imitated the way Jack Knowledge brushed his hair aside, and I couldn't help laughing.

"Sit down, dipstick," Paige snapped. She was the oldest and thought she was the smartest. She got straight A's in school and wore her hair in a beehive. "Listen!"

"I usually wait until there's nothing left to wear," Jack explained. "Then I do a marathon load. I take it down to that shopping plaza off Route 5, the one with the penny arcade. I play pinball while I wait."

Mama laughed, high and sharp. A nervous laugh.

"Listen, how much do I owe you?"

"No, no," she said, and I could picture her waving her hand, or else the hamburger spatula. "Forget it."

"Don't be ridiculous. You've got three kids to support."

"I wanted to do it. I have this thing about clutter."

"I'll add five dollars to my next rent check."

"It wasn't that much."

"Probably more," he said.

"No, five is plenty. Well, it's up to you."

She was good at making nothing out of something, but he was even better at making sure things were fair. I liked him all of a sudden, but the feeling didn't last.

❋

We didn't return to the Cape that summer like my sisters and I had hoped. Mama waited until the day after school let out to tell us. "We're staying here." Jo had a fit and ran off into the woods and didn't come back until dinner time, and even then, she wouldn't talk. She hid in our room, lying facedown on the bed. After dinner, Mama brought her some ice cream, but she refused to even turn her head. Mama left the bowl on the bedside table and joined the rest of us down in the living room where we were watching "The Addams Family."

"I've had it with her," Mama said.

When it came time for bed, I took off my playclothes and put on my nightie without saying a word. Jo's face was buried in her pillow, arms limp at her sides, her fingers curled like the legs of some dead animal. It was still light out, laundromat-warm air wafting through our bedroom windows, carrying in the scent of fresh-mown grass and green from the trees. My feet were dirty from playing outdoors, but Mama had forgotten all about my bath. I climbed into bed, then started bouncing up and down on the mattress.

"C'mon, Jo," I said, trampoleening. "They're outside. We can make as much noise as we want!"

She pretended not to hear.

Landing hard, I said, "Mama's outdoors with Jack Knowledge, drinking beer."

Mama had never drunk beer in her life until Jack Knowledge came to live with us. Usually, she either sipped white wine or had a vodka tonic at the end of an especially hard week. She called beer "that stupid jock drink," but now she crumpled the cans and tossed them in the trash, hollering, "Bingo!"

Jo still didn't move a muscle. I slipped out of bed. Her face was mashed up against her pillow, her skin very pale. "Jo? You okay?" I touched her wrist. "Hey, Jo?"

Suddenly, she growled at me, digging her fingers in the air. I screamed, and she burst out laughing.

"What's so funny?" I backed away, reaching the safety of my own bed.

"You! You looked so scared!"

"I thought you were dead." I stared out the window at the far lights of town shimmering dimly in the early evening air. A pale mist stroked the horizon. Insects spun aimlessly outside my window, hurtling themselves against the screen. "I wish we could go to the Cape," I said, and Jo stopped laughing.

"I hate Mama. She doesn't care about Dad anymore."

"Yes, she does," I said without conviction.

"All she cares about is Jack. Stupid ol' Jack Knowledge. Hippie shithead."

I rolled around to face her, sheets already warm from their contact with my body. "I wish we could go to the Cape this summer and find Dad. Maybe he's a hermit, living on the beach? Maybe he's got amnesia?"

"That's dumb," she said, but waited to hear what I'd say next.

"What if some lady or something . . . . some rich lady . . . . found him washed up on the beach and took him to her house and nursed him back to health? That kinda thing happens all the time. And so he lost his memory, but now he's living with her. He's forgotten that he already has a family. So we've got to remind him!"

"Amnesia," she said softly.

I picked the dirt between my toes. Outside, I could hear Mama laughing. She and Jack had pulled two lawn chairs up beside the well house where they could look out over the back field. Mama usually wore shorts, showing off her tan; but tonight, she was wearing the same calico dress she'd practically lived in all last summer on the Cape, before our father disappeared.

"And then one day, we'll find him wandering along the beach, collecting seashells. 'Dad!' we'll scream, only he won't recognize us. He'll give us this blank look. And then we'll give him a great big kiss, and he'll finally remember!"

"What about Mama?"

"She'll kiss him, too, and his eyes will go all soft and he'll say, 'Beetle!'" I couldn't help it; I laughed. Beetle was Dad's pet name for her.

"Wouldn't that be great?" Jo held her legs in the air, fanning her toes wide. Then she collapsed, bedsprings squeaking. "But it's just a dream. Dad's dead."

"How d'you know?" I asked.

"Mama said so."

"They never found him."

"What about those ashes?"

"Could've been anybody's."

"No, they couldn't," Paige said from the hallway, and it shocked me to realize she'd been listening. Through the crack in the door, I could see her baby doll pajamas and her ugly beehive hairdo. It was teased way up. Jo said if she didn't wash it soon, she'd get bugs. "Why don't you grow up, Mimi? They found Dad on the beach the next morning. *Drowned.*" The way she said it made me want to cry; it was as if she didn't care.

"Mama!" Jo screamed. "Paige's spying on us!"

"Am not."

Jo hopped out of bed and kicked the door open, and Paige shrieked. Before she could get away, Jo grabbed at her chest. "Titties!"

"Ignoramus!" Paige ran back into her room and slammed the door shut. I heard Mama laugh again, and then Jack Knowledge said something, probably one of his dumb jokes. He was always saying corny things, like, "I see, said the blind man, as he picked up his hammer and saw . . . ."

Jo made sure our door was closed. "Listen," she said, climbing into bed with me, sharing her half-melted coffee ice cream. "I'm gonna run away. Wanna come? We can catch the bus to South Yarmouth."

"But our savings is gone. Mama spent it."

"What d'you mean, she spent it?"

"For Christmas. Didn't she tell you?"

"No."

"Well, my savings book says oh-oh-oh."

"I'm gonna find out what mine says." She hopped out of bed and tore out of the room.

"Hey, wait!" I chased after her.

✳

Mama and Jack Knowledge were lying side by side on yellow lawn chairs out back, four beer cans crumpled in the grass between them. The sun had set, but it was still light out. When we passed the kitchen window, Jo stuck out her tongue. "If he becomes our stepfather, I'll puke."

We tiptoed into the TV room. Jo moved like a robot, smooth and jerky at the same time. She poked through the papers and bills in Mama's desk, while I kept a lookout.

"Here it is!" She opened her savings book, and her lips puckered. "Nothing," she whispered. "I had forty-five dollars. Now it's gone!"

"Just like I said."

"Don't be a know-it-all." She tucked the savings book back into its cubbyhole, then found Paige's and frowned. "Zilch."

We tiptoed back to the window. Mama was laughing as if she'd just heard the funniest joke in the world.

Jack was talking. "And so he said, 'Is the mayor there?' And I said, 'I think you have a wrong number.' And he said, 'Listen . . . . listen, have you ever heard the word *palanumbular?*' And I said, 'What?' Man, this guy's really lost it."

They both laughed, and Jack reached for Mama's elbow, and she let his fingers linger on her skin. Jo turned to me, suddenly inspired. "I'm going up to his room. Wanna come?"

"But we can't."

"Why not?"

"Because . . . . Mama would kill us."

"She won't find out." Jo pointed. "Look, they're drunk."

I stared for a long time at the beer can in Mama's hand. "Okay," I said finally.

✳

Jack's room was a mess—dirty clothes everywhere, books and magazines scattered across the floor, crumpled blankets draped over the only chair. Jo and I exchanged frightened looks. It was roasting in the attic, even with the fan on, and smelled of dust and dead wasps.

I stood guard, while Jo explored. First she peeked under the bed. Then she opened all the bureau drawers and rummaged around. She found a single, bright red sock and tucked it in her shorts pocket. She found a loose button and took that, too. She made her way across the room, stepping barefoot over knots of shirts and a prickly hairbrush on its back. She fished through a glass ashtray, selected the butt of a silver cigarette and held it to her nose. "Yuck, stinks!"

I clamped my hand over my mouth, trying not to laugh. My whole body kept shivering. She went through the pockets of his pants and found a photograph of a lady riding a horse. We examined the picture together, wondering who it could be.

"His sister, maybe?"

"An old girlfriend."

"D'you think Mama knows?"

We heard a sound and stiffened. Downstairs, the front door slammed shut, and Mama's laughter traveled up the staircase.

"Let's go." Jo put the photograph away, shut the dresser drawers and we hurried down the attic stairs, hearts beating in our throats. We skidded into our room just as Mama and Jack Knowledge reached the foot of the stairs.

"Shhh!" she hissed. "The girls are sleeping."

"No, they're not!" Jack hollered. "I hear little mice scurrying around up there!"

"Shhh!" Mama laughed helplessly.

We lay stiff in our beds, waiting for her to come check on us, but she never did. She went directly to the bathroom at the end of the hall, while Jack Knowledge scratched on the door. "Hurry, Beth, hurry!"

Jo's lips curled with disgust. "Big babies."

✳

"The same old rules don't apply anymore," Jack Knowledge said. His face was long and pointed, delicate veins throbbing under the skin of his temples. His hair was stretched behind his skull in a knot, making his medium-sized ears stick out. A couple of long blonde hairs strayed from his ear holes, hairs that caught the candlelight. I focused on those lit-up hairs while he rambled on about the rules not applying anymore.

"Black isn't 'colored,' white isn't superior, even men and women . . . ." He looked at Mama and smiled without showing any teeth.

"Men and women are no longer on opposite sides of the fence."

Mama picked at the peas on her plate. We were trying not to make any noise while we ate, since our chewing and swallowing bothered Jack. "Enthusiastic eaters," he'd called us the week before. Paige sat up straight in her chair, hardly touching her hamburger. Every time Jack finished a sentence, she'd nod her head, making the little bow crowning her beehive tremble.

"Young or old, black or white," Jack shrugged, "none of these differences matters anymore. Society's headed in a new direction, a utopian, egalitarian direction."

"Amen." Mama put her fork down and wiped her mouth, smiling into her napkin.

"Take homosexuality," Jack said, and Jo rolled her eyes. "Who says it's wrong to prefer your own sex? That's the old way of thinking. It's up to the individual. Do your own thing, long as nobody gets hurt. Am I right?"

"Right," Mama agreed. Her paper napkin was streaked with red from her lipstick. She left her half-eaten hamburger on her plate and folded her hands in her lap, satisfied.

"Everybody's got a right to do his or her own thing. Without interference. That's what makes America truly beautiful. Not that this country's perfect. Far from it."

"Look at the war," Paige said, pushing her glasses back up her nose and gesturing vaguely toward the TV set.

"Exactly." Jack Knowledge smacked the table with the flat of his palm, making the silverware jump. Jo nudged my leg with hers, mouthing the word 'Exactly,' and I covered my mouth and coughed.

"Exactly," Jack repeated, "the undeclared 'war' in Vietnam. What're we doing there? Can anybody tell me?" He looked around at each of us. My jaw locked; it was like a quiz.

"Who knows?" Mama said, brushing Jack's remark away. She laughed.

"Exactly." He pointed his butter knife at her. "Who knows?"

Everyone relaxed. Mama got up to clear the table, and Paige and Jo and I helped. It was as if nobody wanted to get stuck with him; he might start asking more questions.

✳

Jack Knowledge came from a small Vermont town called Berryton, but he'd been all over the world—New Mexico, Greece, Canada. He taught English at the community college, but his plan was to write a great novel, a novel about the Age of Aquarius. "Right now," he said, "while I'm living it!" We heard him typing late at night in the attic room. Mama had loaned him her old manual Royal, and the clunk of keys hitting the roller kept us awake for hours.

Whenever Jack stayed up late typing his novel, we'd switch on the light between our beds and talk, or else rest our ears against our transistor radios, listening to the same station together. "Oldies but moldies," Jo called the Frankie Avalon-Annette Funicello duets.

We talked mostly about Jack and Mama. I'd start by saying how much I hated him. "He hogs the bathroom. He picks his nose and wipes it on the couch! He wastes water, but Mama never says a thing."

"The well house pump's always going," Jo agreed. "Once I saw him scratching his . . . . you know."

"What? His what?"

" . . . . front part."

"Yuck! Are you serious?"

"As if I wasn't even there."

"Disgust-o!"

"And that cootie way he looks at Mama." Jo made a dopey grin.

"She never has time for us anymore. She hates us."

Jo leaned against one elbow, our bedside lamp casting long shadows down her face, making her seem old. In a month, she'd be ten. "He painted the table in the attic pitch black."

"Did he?"

"Yeah. Remember when Mama made him those black curtains? She said it was to shut out the light, but you should see. He's turning everything black up there."

"He can't just paint things over without asking."

"Yes, he can. He can do whatever he likes."

We pouted for a while, thinking about all the things Mama never let us do.

Jo's little finger reached out to scratch her cheek. "It's like that Rolling Stones song, y'know? 'Painted Black.'"

"Yeah," I said. "How's it go?"

Jo became animated, tapping her fingers on the bedside table between us. "Na-nah-nah-nah-nah-nah . . . . nah-nah-nah painted black . . . . No colors nah-nah-nah, they na-nah painted black . . . ."

"Oh yeah." We paused a moment, trying to hear whether or not the typing had stopped, but the thumping of depressed keys rained down on us.

"And don't you hate the way he tells us stuff? Like he's our teacher or something."

"He won't shut up." Jo scratched her chest through her nightie. Last winter, Mama had made us matching nighties with matching ruffled panties. She'd picked out the fabric herself, strobing green-on-orange dots. "Op art!" she'd said, straight pins poking out her mouth.

"We've got to do something, Mimi. We don't want Mama to marry him, do we?"

"No!" I said, horrified.

"We've got to make her see what a jerk he is."

"How?"

"Lemme think." Jo tapped her chin, while I waited silently; I had no idea how to get rid of him. We fell asleep before we could figure it out.

✳

Jo and I spent many sleepless nights discussing Jack's short-comings while he typed his great American novel. But despite our plans, whenever daylight rolled around, the best we could think of was making fun of him behind his back. If he farted in the bathroom, we'd make farting sounds with our lips. Mama always scolded us, saying we weren't being polite. She never asked us what we thought of Jack living there. She never asked us anything.

I'd never seen Mama so happy, not since before our father disappeared. Last summer, he jumped off the end of a jetty and disappeared into the churning water. It was night, pitch black, and we ran with her to the concession stand to call the police. Later Paige told us they found the body the following day, but I didn't believe it. A boxful of ashes, that wasn't my father.

Paige spent most of her days locked in her room, listening to music or else doing her homework. Sometimes Jo and I would ambush her coming out of the bathroom. We'd tug on her towel, and she'd scream at us as we snuck peeks at her strange new curves.

Mama was tan from working outdoors in her garden. Her hair was growing long, and she kept it out of her face with a dark blue headband. She didn't change the color of her lipstick, even though lighter shades were in; her smile had such bounce to it, such shine, it really didn't matter. All her new dresses zipped up the back. She didn't wear anything on her long tanned legs but her leather sandals.

Mama worked at the bakery during the afternoons, then came home and made dinner for the five of us every night. Whenever we offered to help, she said, "No problem!" so brightly, we finally gave up asking.

At dinner, Jack would drink two beers with his meal and fill us in on the state of the world. Once in a while, he'd mention Mary Jane, and I wondered if that was the lady in the picture that Jo and I had seen in his room. "Before Mary Jane," he'd say, "there was very little understanding about the far East." He'd shoot Mama a small, almost invisible wink, and she'd change the subject immediately. She always seemed flustered whenever he mentioned his old girlfriend, and I thought I understood why.

Jack knew Jo and I didn't like him. He tried to ignore it when we giggled at the stupid things he said, but we could see his irritation in the way he kept rearranging his fork and knife on the placemat and shifting around in his seat. No matter how hard he tried, he couldn't seem to get comfortable in our worn-out furniture.

Finally, Mama took us aside. "You girls are being cruel, and I want you to stop."

"What d'you mean?" Jo asked, all innocence.

"You know damn well." She leaned forward, twisting a dish towel between her hands. "All this snickering and poking fun. Jack's a nice guy. Why can't you be nice?"

"Sorry," I said, giving in, but Jo made a fist.

"He uses the bathroom longer than anybody else!"

"He's allowed. He pays for it."

That didn't stop Jo. "He leaves his underwear all over the attic so I can't play with my trains."

"You shouldn't be up there. That's Jack's space now. He deserves a right to privacy, he pays for it."

"I'd pay, too, if I had any savings left," Jo snarled, catching Mama off guard.

"I couldn't help it, Jo." Her voice was strained. "I had to pay for that fancy Christmas I gave you girls."

"You didn't have to give us any fancy Christmas! We weren't expecting one."

Paige, who'd been sitting in the other room, turned her head in our direction.

"You mean you didn't like it? Is that what you're saying?" Mama was on the verge of tears now.

"Not if it means you can go around stealing our money any time you want!"

Mama looked shocked; her eyes glazed over and her forehead flushed. I felt invisible standing there beside them, as if I were watching soldiers snipe at one another on the TV set. My chest became hotter with every breath I took, and the circular overhead fluorescent lamp glowed behind Mama's head like a halo.

"It wasn't yours to begin with. I put that money in there! I can do whatever I please. And if you can't even appreciate what I did for you girls last Christmas, I . . . . I don't know what."

She turned away from us, still wringing the dish towel, and headed toward the stairs, but Jo followed her.

"Jack stays up all night long, typing, and we can't sleep!" she shouted. I was glad Jack wasn't anywhere near the house. Even from his attic room, he would've heard.

Mama turned. "Why didn't you tell me?"

For the first time, Jo seemed at a loss for words. Her shoulders slumped under Dad's old gray T-shirt.

"Because you wouldn't've done anything!" I said, surprised at the strength of my voice. "You like Jack more than you like us."

"That's not true."

"You're in love with him, aren't you?" I accused her. "You're going to marry him."

She blushed, patting her cheeks with the dish towel. "Of course not. Where'd you get such an idea? He's just a boarder, that's all."

Paige came into the kitchen wearing Bermuda shorts over her bathing suit like a beauty queen.

"You two are always laughing and drinking beer together. You never used to drink beer, Mama." Suddenly I wanted to cry. All those sleepless nights underneath Jack's typewriter seemed to have gathered into a bitter lump in my throat. "You never used to watch TV."

"I still don't."

"Leave her alone," Paige said, leaning against the kitchen doorway. Without her glasses on, she was almost pretty. Grown up. "Jack hasn't hurt you. He hasn't hurt anybody. He's real smart and real nice, only you guys are too dumb to know it."

"That's enough, Paige," Mama said.

"Mama, you put up with those two babies, and then they turn against you, and you still protect them!"

"I said, that's enough."

I could barely breathe, the silence was so embarrassing.

"I loved your father. . . . It's terrible what happened to us," Mama said. "I miss him very much. But now he's gone, and we have to get on with our lives. I'm sorry about the noise, girls," she said. "I'll talk to Jack. I wish you'd told me earlier."

From the doorway, Paige stuck out her tongue.

"I love you all very much." Her voice was sharp. "Okay?"

"Okay," I murmured.

"Now, out. I've got dishes to do."

Paige's hips swayed as she walked away from us. "Babies," she said, loud enough for us to hear.

✳

That night, there was no typing in the attic. Jo and I stared at each other, eyes filled with expectation . . . . but Jack's fingers never hit the keyboard once, and soon we fell asleep. I dreamt we were staring out the living room windows at the sea. Enormous waves engulfed the house, beating against the windowpanes. In my dream, Mama kept trying to convince us nothing was wrong. There was absolutely nothing to worry about, she said.

On Saturday, Mama paid for the three of us to go to the movies. Paige spent a long time getting ready. Jo and I waited outside her room, scratching on her door with our fingernails, making her shriek. When she finally came out, she was wearing a purple minidress with a pixie collar and short sleeves. We tugged at the hem of her dress. "Too short! Too short!"

Jack Knowledge dropped us off at the only movie theater in town and drove away. "Yellow Submarine" was playing. In the lobby, Jo and Paige started fighting over the money Mama had given us. Jo said, "I want a large popcorn and a box of Pom-Poms and a ginger ale."

"Brat!" Paige smacked Jo's arm, leaving a red spot.

Jo slapped Paige so hard, she went flying across the soiled lobby carpet and ran screaming into the ladies' room.

"C'mon," Jo said.

"Where we going?"

"Home."

We left the theater, and after a minute, Paige came tearing out after us. Her face was red and swollen, and I thought she was going to punch Jo's lights out. But instead, the three of us just walked home together in silence.

It took us almost an hour. The front door was unlocked and the house was empty. "Where are they?" Paige asked in a soft voice.

"Let's go upstairs," Jo whispered.

We stood in Paige's bedroom and looked down over the back yard where we spotted them in a far field. They were lying on a blanket, having a picnic. Except they weren't eating anything. It was strange to see Mama lying so still, while Jack ran his hands through her hair.

"I've got an idea," Jo said, and we followed her up the attic stairs.

We started picking up shirts and underwear from the floor, gathering armfuls of clothes. We took them into Jack Knowledge's room where all the furniture was painted black, and the air was stuffy. Jo removed the fan from the window, opened the window wide, and we tossed everything outside. Shirts and underpants drifted like tiny parachutes, landing on the bushes below, drifting into our mother's flower garden, floating across the gravel path. We found Jack's unfinished novel and threw that out, too. We craned our necks as pages fluttered across the road.

✳

Three months later, he was gone. Our mother survived, eventually taking a job in an art gallery and seeing the three of us through college. Now she's curator of the Lincoln Art Museum in Pearl River and has a boyfriend who sleeps over.

But I still recall Mama's sadness after Jack Knowledge left, the long nights she spent sewing in front of the TV, or else looking at the stars through a pair of binoculars on the back porch. And I blame myself for her pain—I blame us all.

I'll never forget the look in her eyes when she saw what we'd done. She and Jack spotted the snowfall of clothes and ran down from the field and across the lawn, picking up pages. Mama's hair was tangled. "What . . . .?" Her face registered shock, and then betrayal. She looked at each of us, and my hands trembled on the window frame. "Girls," she said, "oh girls."

Her voice was soft and so forlorn, I wanted to cry out, "I'm sorry, Mama!" My eyes burned with shame and my stomach ached, and suddenly I hated my sisters, hated what we'd done to her. But then the air went out of my lungs, and all I could say was, "It's Dad."

"What?" she asked, her face a child's. "What?"

Americans

I never met your junkie husband, Ramona. I moved in after he died and watched you grieve. You told me all about him while you combed your frizzy blonde hair and rearranged shimmering tubes of makeup in precise rows on the shag rug— mossy green eye shadow, cinnamon-spice lip gloss, raspberry blush. You sat beside me on the couch, clutching your knees to your chest and talking while your baby cried and groped his way across the room to be with you. Poor Lennie, fatherless snail, smacked the black furniture with his luminous wet hands, pink threads dangling from his mouth; he slapped wooden chair seats and plastic table legs and dirty splintered orange crates, taking one uncertain step after another on those stocky, rashed legs, his small face torn with grief as if it were a latex mask, all pink and swirled in its own pain.

"Bad boy!" you said, scooping him up like dirty underwear from the floor and hugging him to your chest. You were only nineteen, too young to have a kid, sixteen when you met Ansel—the husband who beat you and stole neon Budweiser signs from the neighborhood bars, who slept through all the feedings and had affairs with other women—beautiful women, you told me, unlike yourself with your crooked nose and uneven eyes the color of partially roasted coffee beans, bitter. And your skinny arms and legs, boy's feet with splayed toes, and that residue of acne covering your face and upper back like a smooth pink fungus. I could only make it out, Ramona, if I stood real close, but you felt like a beggar in your leprous skin and avoided brightly lit places—supermarkets, beauty shops.

We were roommates in West Hollywood where all the fags lived, you said, a good neighborhood with plenty of cafes. You shredded whole boxes of Kleenex and bit your wrists, sat Indian-style on the rug and let the baby cry. Your breasts often bothered you, and you rubbed them absently while you gazed out the French windows at the overbright sky. The state sent you checks, and you drank Tropicana orange juice as you contemplated what you'd spend your money on. You mostly gave it away—to friends, relatives—and bought the baby expensive toys, his bedroom knee-deep in multi-colored furs and plastics.

I wanted to be an actress. After three weeks in L.A., I landed a job at Universal as somebody's secretary, and every night when I came home, you offered to rub my feet, digging your long thumbpads into my sweaty arches and telling me about your life. "Ansel and I used to sell coke, downs, Black Beauties. We'd go to the Vermont, this crappy old diner. I met one of my regulars there, a real slick black guy with a harelip. One day he asked, could he see my ring? My grandmother's wedding band, the only thing I brought with me from home. I didn't want to show him, but you know how persuasive some people can be. I was young and real naive, and I handed it over. He screwed it onto his pinkie finger, said pretty. I said, okay, give it back, but he didn't give it back, he just walked out of there. That night, when I told Ansel, he hit me. He was always hitting me. I felt so ugly around him."

Ramona, I found you beautiful, with all that coiling hair, your bittersweet eyes and the flexible curves of your mouth. Did you know how much I admired you? Survivor of your drug-crazed youth? Behind me, a hundred years of farmland and traceable Midwestern ancestry; I was corn and wheat, while you walked the street on your skinny bored legs, belly full of baby. You begged on street corners and rolled drunks, ripped off supermarkets—apples, M&Ms, whatever you could get your spindly fingers on—while I stayed home and watched *Bewitched* like a good little girl; and you were rolling nickels into blue paper holders, picking seeds out of homegrown pot.

I lived with you for six months, Ramona; we twisted our beer cans into the shag rug to root them and sunbathed in the broad sweep of light spilling in through the French windows, our skin turning the color of coffee mixed with cream. You said, "We lived on Normandie in this tiny unfurnished studio. There were silverfish in the bathroom, and we didn't have a stick of furniture, not even a bed. So we went to Zayre's and stole two rubber air mattresses—you know, the kind they float in pools? Well, before long, they both sprang leaks, and so every morning, we'd be lying flat on our backs on the floor. And every night, we blew them up again."

You worked as an usherette at the Cinerama, saw *Top Gun* about a hundred times. Late at night, as you waited for the bus, strange men in expensive-looking cars rolled down their windows and propositioned you; and once, an old guy in a ten-gallon hat, Indian tiger tattooed on his hairy arm, circled the block a dozen times, calling to you. "C'mere, girl! C'mere, little lady! C'mere an' gimme a blow job! Fuck me good!" he said, spit mixing with his words, all mixed up, and you were tempted to go because he offered you a hundred dollars.

Ramona, why did you think so poorly of yourself? You, with your strong sharp face, black sunglasses in your shirt pocket, baby at your breast, iridescent eye shadow smeared across your long eyelids? You absently jiggled keys in your hand, read *Playboy*, made a muscle and told me to squeeze, and I did, a firm warm bulge. You wore ratty T-shirts and antique vests, silk blouses, stiff white painter's pants and bunched khaki trousers with short silver zippers over each pocket and horizontally down each cuff. Taking pictures, you hid your ragged hair beneath the brim of a black fedora. And the photographs! A saggy-faced bag lady picking her nose under the crucifix of the Hollywood and Vine signs; plastic Santas with bulbous red noses propped against a backdrop of sea and sand and poinsettia; the baby in his shriveled newborn skin.

Lennie was always howling, and you'd pick him up and repeat his name softly until his sobs shrank to gasps, little expectancies, and you'd carry him out into the living room with you, into the bright sunshine, where he'd bunch up his tragic face. Daddy was a junkie, you cooed while he gazed at you, captivated by your tone. Daddy's dead and gone, you sang.

You ate bargain-brand English muffins, scraping the spotty green mold off the bottoms, and drank Kool-Aid while the baby ran around naked, touching everything. "My husband stole people's jewelry and TV sets and brought them home," you confessed, "and hid them under the bed. I'd ask him, 'What'd you do? What'd you do?' And he'd look at me with tears in his eyes and promise never to do it again. It was always the last time, and I always believed him. Ansel had red hair and green eyes; he was crazy, a crazy mother. And the next day, he'd go out and hock all that shit and buy smack. Have you ever seen anybody strung out on smack? They start to nod their heads, like this, and a funny smell comes from their mouths. I'd know that smell anywhere."

And once the baby stumbled toward you, landing in your lap and grabbing your hoop earring; you stood up screaming, lips a puddle of surprise, blue eyes wide, big white teeth, and the baby started crying, too, earring caught in his fist like a bloody fishhook. Blood ran down the side of your neck and underneath your chin, and you swore and shivered while the baby shrieked, and I ran into the bathroom for bandages and iodine.

Ramona, you were so sad all the time. Beaten down, one of life's favorite victims, you called yourself.

But then, Edie came into your life and changed everything. Tall city girl with long legs, so athletic-looking for someone who hated to get up just to change channels on the TV. Her square face was boyish and her pale green eyes were like the flesh of a ripe avocado. Edie, with that insane temper and vaguely Southern accent—even though she was from Milwaukee—because she had this desire to be a cowboy. The way she walked, always stalking her prey.

Ramona, I used to picture you two lying on your queen-size bed with the spool headboard—clinging together, black and yellow hair tangled over the pillows. I imagined you making love, your long fingers gripping the polished spooled bars of the headboard.

For a while, you were happy, and the baby got fatter, his legs two spherical stalks, his stomach protruding like the belly of a starving child on one of those TV commercials. You liked to hold him by the fleshy arms and stand him on your knees, watch him stagger and sway as he tested his legs, pockets of fat bulging above the knee-caps. He tossed his arms in quirky arcs and smiled, tips of his new teeth like glistening barnacles breaking through the pink and healthy gums. His eyes were deep blue wells I could toss pennies into.

One day, the three of us went to the beach and grabbed hand-fuls of stale Wonder Bread from a plastic bag. Gulls drifted on pow-erful currents of air that whipped our hair back in our faces, gulls braced like white kites—you could almost feel the tug of the string. They turned their suspicious yellow eyes on us, opened their beaks to let out that eerie, reverberating cry. And we tossed handfuls of crumbs like packed snow, and they snatched at the bread, barely moving, their necks making graceful arcs in the air.

It wasn't long before Edie was bullying you. I listened at the door and heard you sob, Edie's dark voice crashing over you, and I pounded on the wall, wanting to pound you both into silence, flat as hammered metal. And later on, you told me to mind my own business or else find another place to live; do you remember? How my eyes took you in? So startled? How they rounded in disbelief? Do you realize how much I wanted to protect you? I couldn't be-lieve you wanted such a life, couldn't believe you'd grown up in a place where people stabbed each other and OD'd and stole things. And my heart raced as I promised I'd leave you two alone, my mis-take.

There were good times between the fights and bitterness, be-tween the jealousies; we took long walks around Hollywood, past hookers in their Frederick's getups and pimps with their aqua satin shirts and flashy smiles, past tourists from Utah—potato hips, sweaty upper lips, cameras always clicking. And once, some rough teenage boys from Inglewood or Bakersfield followed us out of the movies and flicked their lit cigarettes at our ankles. Edie's face flamed as she slowed her pace, her slender fists readied, and one of the boys tapped you on the shoulder, Ramona, and said, "Hey, you a dyke or somethin'?" in a high whiny voice, and you turned to him and said, "I'm an American, just like you." And the boys laughed uneasily while Edie tried to stare one of them down; she was shaking in her cowboy boots, livid, and they swung in a wide circle around us, as if we were diseased, leaving the echo of their derisive laughter and smoke from their cigarillos in the summer air.

Edie swallowed her bile and I knew that, later, she'd take it out on you. That night at Sadie's, you two held hands under the table and sipped your sloe gin fizzes. From my seat, I could see the entire place, the front room with its vinyl-padded stools, the curving bar, the front door and windows with their neon signs—Schlitz spelled backwards, Budweiser blinking, ice-blue. Women sat at the bar, leather pants darkly gleaming, their feet hooked around the rungs of their stools. They slouched over their drinks and gazed blearily up at the color TV. A fight was on. Blaring rock music came out of a jukebox that looked like an old Buick, one of those buttery-cornered kinds with tubes of colored light framing the window and gigantic selector knobs. A silver disco ball hung from the ceiling, just for laughs, you said.

You told me over the wet table, "My husband used to keep a gun. I didn't want a gun in the house, not with the baby, so I told him to get rid of it. And I thought he did. He had this beautiful maroon jacket he used to wear once in a while, and he said, 'When I die, I want you to bury me in this jacket.' I hated it when he talked that way. And one day he came home and disappeared into the bathroom, and when he came out, he had the gun. He slipped it in the pocket of this white linen jacket he had on. 'Where are you going with that?' I said, but he wouldn't tell me.

"I tried to stop him, but he told me to stay put. Only I didn't stay put. I followed him out onto the street, into this shitty little bar where he met somebody I didn't recognize. And then, as I was standing in the doorway, I watched him pull the gun. And the guy grabs it away and shoots him. Right in the chest. And there was blood all over his chest, covering his white jacket, so much blood. And everybody screamed and ran out the door, and I bent over him and knew he was dead. And I couldn't help thinking he'd get buried in his maroon jacket after all."

Edie looked around as if she'd heard the story before, then got up and went over to the bar. She started talking to a very beautiful girl, and I watched your eyes, Ramona; they lost all hope. They raged.

Edie and the girl started dancing, and you asked me to dance, too, but I didn't want to. The bar was full of women, and they frightened me. You begged me to dance with you, just once, just this once, you said. In the bar's darkness, your acne scars disappeared and your skin was washed of color, your narrow face almost vampirish.

"Dance with me, Deborah!" you begged. "Please, just this once."

And I gave in; we slid out of the booth, joined the others on the floor, and you leaned toward me, our cheeks almost touching, and said, "This is the first gay bar I ever went to. Edie brought me here, the week we became lovers. I was scared shitless. It was like finally admitting to myself what I was." And your eyes glittered as you said that, and you glanced over at Edie—absorbed, revolving with the beauty—and your heart crumpled. You rotated your bare brown shoulders, stretched your arms straight up, snapped your fingers to the beat, and I got drunk just watching.

Ramona, I should've stopped you. Edie and the beauty kept on dancing, their two sets of arms, sinuous as snakes, revolved in the air above their heads, the colored lights changing their complexions, two chameleons. And you were preoccupied, absorbed in your war, intent on hurting Edie as much as she was hurting you, and so you laughed loudly at nothing; you cupped my face and laughingly kissed me, tongue lapping at my front teeth. And I hated you just then, even as I rested my hands on your hips and felt the solidity of your body, your swaying sense of balance. You laughed again, vacantly, a lost teenager at some high school dance, and flashed a Hollywood smile and spun me around, your feet stamping to the faster beat of a new song; like a Spanish dancer, you clicked invisible castanets and swam around me, flicking your ragged straw-colored hair in my face, and Edie, glancing over, threw you a bemused smile. She took her partner by the arm and they walked off together into the darkest corner.

"Did you see that?" you cried, furious. "She put her arm around her as if she owned her! She thinks she owns everyone."

And I became suddenly terrified; I wanted you back, back to myself, needed you to protect me from this, and I sat down and drank the flat beer while you followed Edie and her new lover into the darkest corner. I couldn't look, I was sick of watching, so I went to the john and nearly passed out, studied my own face in the mirror while I ran my finger through a garden of grease.

And when I came out, you had your hands around her wrists. You screamed, "Go fuck her! Go ahead! Fuck yourself sick!" And Edie looked at me accusingly, her eyes filled with a convict's hate, as if she had absolutely no way of stopping the anger that was welling inside her, or even of toning it down, and she threw you on the floor, Ramona, while the other women cleared a space, and jumped on you like some predatory dog—she would've eaten you alive. She jerked your arm back so far you screamed in pain. Your face was meant for pain, Ramona, the way the lines fell into place. And you scuttled forward over the slippery floor while two others held Edie back, and she bit great chunks out of the air, spitting them at us, and the beauty disappeared into the shadows.

You tore your keys out of your purse, and we ran for the car, panting; you slipped on the slick tile of the doorstep, scraping your elbow, and shook the key in its greasy lock, and we slammed the doors, locked them shut, rolled up the windows, our humid breath fogging the glass. Edie tore from the bar like an attack dog, hurling insults, strung out on her own heady fury, her cowboy rage; she stumbled to the car while you tried to start it, hands trembling, and whispered swear words under your breath, like a Catholic schoolgirl—softly and in alphabetical order, "Damn . . . hell . . . shit . . ."— methodical as prayer.

Edie hurled her beer bottle at the windshield, a long crack spewing across the glass like a silver string of spilt milk. Then she jumped on the hood and tried to rip the antenna out by its welded root. "Fucking bitch!" she screamed, her face a blur, a drunken palette. "I'll kill you and your fucking little cunt of a friend!" And I knew that if she'd had a gun, she'd've shot us.

You backed out of the long driveway while I sat beside you, shivering, and Edie pounded the windshield with her blue fist; it slid sluglike down the glass, and she screamed directly at you, her face a few feet away, her hoarse voice muffled, and you swung the car out onto the road while she clung to the antenna, screaming, her long body swinging over the hood like a rubber rag in a car wash. I could hear you breathing.

You stepped on the gas and I hissed, "Watch it!" as if I could prevent what was about to happen, what I clearly saw coming, and the car squealed and veered and let out vapors—burnt rubber and Seagram's—and Edie rolled off the hood like a bag of potatoes, her eyes still reaching for you behind the glass. She careened off the edge of the car, her screams thinning out as we sped toward the highway, into the black neon-lit night, trailing pieces of her anger after us like the tin cans of a wedding car.

You said, "I'm just so sick of being abused."

"But what if she's hurt? Maybe we should turn back?"

"I hope she's dead."

That night, you fed yourself pills from a velvet-lined box. "They know me at the bar," you said, "what if I really hurt her?" You tilted your head to drink, Adam's apple jutting like the whitened knuckle of a flexed finger. "She'll come after me, Deborah. Why do I have such bad luck?"

And my heart, rocking forward, reached out for you, and I held you because you were so lost. There was no way I could help you, although I still try in my dreams; I go over the events in my mind's eye, black and blue. I used to believe I did it for you, hoping to fix what went wrong with your life. But now, I realize, I do it for me; I need a less tragic way to remember you.

That night you left L.A., left with your baby, stole away in the dark, the apartment was littered with things you could have used—tubes of green eye shadow, money I'd saved from my job, the expensive suitcase you'd stolen. But you left them behind like a bad omen to start someplace new.

Oh, Ramona, I hate to think what's become of you.

The Accident Radio

Adele's high, faltering voice shivered through forty miles of telephone line. "I don't know what to do, Berri. I just lie in bed, listening to him breathe."

"Is he okay?" Berri asked her mother-in-law.

A thoughtful pause. "Still breathing."

"Well, that's good, isn't it?"

"I listen, listen, listen," Adele said, "knowing it could stop any second."

Berri rolled her eyes at Charlie, who dutifully reached for the receiver. It was three in the morning, raining outside.

"Here's Charlie," she said, handing over the phone.

"Go back to sleep, Ma," Charlie said with that soothing tone that occasionally made Berri want to hit him. "He'll be all right."

Charlie's father, Mickie, had recently suffered a minor heart attack while climbing a ladder trying to save a 59-year-old woman trapped inside a burning building. Mickie Smith, a retired structural engineer, had been a volunteer fireman for seven years now, a curiously suicidal pastime, Berri thought, like his excessive smoking. One of his fellow firemen had saved his life by carrying him back down the ladder and administering CPR.

The woman escaped unharmed.

After a week in the hospital, Mickie was sent home to begin life anew, and now Adele's panic attacks were taking on a power all their own, becoming more important even than Mickie's current state of health. It was always like that with Adele; everyone else's tragedy eventually became part of her own ongoing struggle with life.

"No, you aren't," Charlie said now, "you're not being a pest." Berri kicked him, and he playfully grabbed her ankle. "He what? He wants to buy a truck?"

Berri leaned forward and planted silent kisses on her husband's cheek. Adele was Japanese-American, and Charlie had inherited her olive complexion and thick black hair, her tendency to bruise beneath the eyes—eyes which were blue-gray, like his father's. Gary Cooper eyes, Adele called them.

"This weekend?" Charlie looked at Berri.

"No," she hissed, shaking her head.

"Saturday's fine."

Collapsing against her pillow, she let out a low groan.

"Okay, Ma, now get some sleep." He hung up and bumped his head against the headboard.

"Three nights in a row is a little excessive, don't you think?" she said. "Let's unplug the phone."

"But what if there's an emergency?"

"Your father's fine." She ran her hand along his slender, hairy leg. "It's your mother who's the problem."

"If something happens to Dad," Charlie said, "I want to know."

She wrapped her arms around him. They were both sitting up in bed now, naked with the lights on. Berri was determined to get herself pregnant—against this backdrop of melodrama and real illness, she would create new life.

Gently, he pushed her away. "Not now." He played with the flashlight they kept beside the bed, idly switching it on and off and giving a strange cast to his angular face. "Dad wants to buy a Nissan King Cab. He wants to go camping."

"Good. I hope he takes her far, far away." She kissed the warm hollow of his neck.

"I wish you wouldn't do that."

"What, excite you?"

"No, incite me against my family."

Berri rolled over so that she fit snugly into the contours of his body. "You've got to put your foot down, your whole leg. Your beautiful, sexy leg."

"My father's dying, Berri." He stroked her hair.

"No, he's not. The doctors say . . . ."

"I don't give a shit what the doctors say."

Maybe her husband knew something she didn't? At the hospital, the doctors said Mickie Smith could live another thirty years, provided he quit smoking. Admittedly a big if. That must be it; Charlie knew his father would never give up his silver-filtered Shermans.

Now he switched off the light. "Let's get some sleep."

"Charlie . . . ."

"I can't talk about this anymore."

Berri clutched her side of the blanket. They'd once vowed never to go to bed angry, and now Adele was stealing their peace of mind. Berri felt inordinately sad. Her love for her husband had bound her inextricably to this woman in a way she couldn't ignore. She wondered if she'd ever learn to like Adele, or Adele her—or would they always exist in this margin of mutual tolerance?

Charlie pulled hard on the blanket, and she tugged back. Then he grabbed and kissed her. "Let's not fight," he said.

"No. Fighting's a big waste of time."

✳

Adele came toward them with her thin arms outstretched. She was wearing pink stretchpants and a loose white cotton blouse. "Children!" Her chin dug into Berri's neck. Charlie swept her up in his arms, swung her around. "Hi, Mom."

"Aw, sweetie." She giggled like a teenager.

"How's Dad?"

"Come see."

They followed her inside where the air smelled faintly of tobacco and Lysol. The master bedroom upstairs was bright with sunshine, and Adele struggled to open one of the windows, swollen shut from yesterday's rain. Mickie's gray head lay slack against the pillow.

"Hi, Dad." Charlie took his father's hand.

"How ya doin', kiddo?"

Adele whipped the afghan off the foot of the bed, shook it open, and a bunch of get-well cards flew off the bureautop and fluttered around their ankles. Berri bent to pick one up, but Adele snatched it away.

"He's a couch potato now," she said, her voice high and girlish as she rearranged cards on the bureautop.

"Bed potato, you mean."

"Bed bug." She turned to them. "He bit me the other day!"

"Did not."

"Did so!" Her giggle reached like a child's faulty fingering on piano keys.

"Well, you were all over me like a cheap suit."

"Trying to keep your room clean."

"Ha. Some excuse."

"Oh, like you could really do something in your condition!"

Mickie cleared his throat now, a gravelly eruption. He looked worse than he had at the hospital, and Berri began to suspect that maybe her husband and mother-in-law were right . . . . maybe she'd been too optimistic all along.

"Guess what D.A.M. stands for?" Mickie asked.

"What, Dad?"

"Mothers Against Dyslexia." His rubbery face twisted like Donald Duck's, and the laughter exploded from his lungs. Berri was used to seeing him in jeans and flannel shirts, not these faded cowboy pajamas and terrycloth robe with Kleenex stuffed in the pockets. His workboots were tucked underneath the bed, their leather tongues like weather-toughened petals.

Charlie and Adele emitted a couple of nasal honks, and Berri found it strange that the same trait she adored in her husband could be so irritating in her mother-in-law. They both chewed their nails and swallowed the pieces; both were addicted to anything fried; both occasionally burst into that honking laugh of theirs.

"Mickie sits on the toilet seat now," Adele said, "like a girl."

"Chrissakes, Adele. What'd you tell them that for?"

"Well, it's true, isn't it?" Her eyes widened, all innocence.

"And you've got hemorrhoids," Mickie retaliated, making his wife giggle. "She got them giving birth." He held his hands apart the width of a basketball. "My goodness, the things the human body can endure."

Endure. Berri hoped the word applied to Mickie as well.

"My foot slipped at one point," Mickie said, "and I almost broke my neck. Ironic, isn't it? Almost broke my neck right before I had my heart attack. Damn ladder. Straddled it like a horse. Nearly crushed my nuts." He raised his voice to a Minnie Mouse squeak. "That's why I talk like this now!" He snorted, greatly amused.

"Come into the kitchen, guys," Adele said. "I'll make us some coffee."

"Can't have coffee." Mickie patted his chest. "Decaf."

✳

They sat around the kitchen table, Berri, Charlie and Adele, sun heating the backs of their heads and illuminating the bowl of jumbo shrimp Adele was shelling. Berri's elbows kept sticking to the oil-cloth, a cheerful pattern of daisies.

"Can I help?" she asked.

"No, you just sit there." Adele reminded Berri of a chipmunk on the verge of nervous collapse. She hid the dark circles under her eyes with a caky foundation, and her shoulders perpetually sagged. She wore ruffled blouses, cotton pants and wraparound skirts, and her sneakers were the kind without any arch support.

"You two're coming for Christmas, I hope . . . ."

Berri looked at her. "We're spending Christmas with my family this year, Adele. Remember?"

"Well, you can come *around* Christmas, can't you?"

". . . . Yes. Of course, we'll come *around* Christmas."

"Good." She squeezed Berri's hand, leaving a shrimpy wetness.

Now several loud bursts of static emitted from the police radio in the living room—The Accident Radio, Adele called it. Berri remembered the Christmas before last, how the radio had kept them awake all night long while they tried to sleep on the sagging foldout sofa in the living room. Charlie wouldn't ask his parents to turn the volume down, so they'd had to listen to the dispatcher's one-sided conversation all night. "False alarm. Just a smoking basket. Yeah, somebody tossed in a cigarette . . . ." There was a shooting and an automobile accident, and Berri wondered how anybody in their right mind could stand listening to such relentlessly bad news on Christmas Eve. The kitten had pounced all over them, and after they'd finally fallen into a fitful sleep, they were abruptly awakened at four in the morning by the angry sound of a pot hitting the stove. Adele had warned them she'd be getting up early to start the bird, but neither of them had been prepared for the force of her energy, the onslaught of noise. As if she were shaking demons out of the house. It went on for about an hour or so, then the noise stopped, and her silhouette appeared in the doorway. "Sweet dreams," she whispered before tiptoeing up the stairs, leaving them to the staticky hiss of the Accident Radio.

Now Charlie's thick eyebrows furrowed together. "I've never seen him like this before, Mom."

"All he wants to do is lie there." Adele flicked a shrimp tail off the tip of her thumb, and it landed on the daisy-colored oilcloth. "He's supposed to move around the house. Did you see his color? He's no-color. He says I nag him. Me? Can you imagine?"

"He isn't usually so . . . . up front about things," Charlie said.

"You see what a close call can do to a person?"

"Burglary in progress," a voice suddenly blurted from the police radio in the living room, "625 Winchester Ave . . . ."

"That radio," Adele shook her head. "I should sell it or something. He just sits there fuming because he can't go out and rescue somebody. He's gotta be a Big Hero, you know?"

Now Charlie lowered his voice. "Dad's not thinking of chasing anymore fires, is he?"

"I'm almost afraid to ask. Afraid he's given up." Adele wiped some shrimp juice off her chin with the back of her hand, tiny bits of shrimp shell covering her fingers. "I used to ride with him. Sometimes we'd head out at three in the morning. We've got some great pictures."

"Of the fires?" Berri asked.

"I'll show you sometime." She scraped back her chair and carried the bowl to the sink.

※

The next time Adele called, they were in the middle of making love, and Berri answered the phone.

"Is Charlie there? Not that I don't want to talk to you, Berri . . . I shouldn't be asking for him before I've asked you how you are, should I?"

"He's right here, Adele." Berri handed over the phone.

Outside it was raining. Inside, the air was warm and damp, and Charlie's desire was visibly dwindling.

"Mom, you're going to have to stop calling so late from now on," he said, "unless it's important. Well, you're just going to have to stop. It's too late for this kind of conversation."

He hung up and collapsed against his pillow. "How the hell has he put up with her all these years?"

"Unplug the phone."

"What if it's an emergency?"

"Believe me, it won't be," Berri said, tickling her fingers across his chest.

※

It didn't snow that Christmas, although it threatened to. Fog sat thick on the highways, making the billboards appear to float in midair. Mickie and Adele's hometown had a hopeless, lost-in-the-seventies feel. Ugly brick buildings and identical-looking restaurants with names like Cap'n Jack's and Three-D Deli lined the brief Main Street.

The Smith's two-story house was located half a block from a busy intersection. A yellow tricycle, turned on its side, blocked the long rutted driveway. Charlie got out and moved it before parking the car. Then he wrapped his arms around Berri and sighed heavily into her hair. "Merry Christmas, sweetie."

Adele was shaking out a new garbage bag by the back door. She tiptoed through the mud while they collected packages from the back seat. "Happy Christmas!" she cried, flinging her thin arms around them. She was wearing a new wig she'd picked up at the mall. She occasionally liked to change her hair color, she told them. The wig was bright red and curly, and her new pink lipstick gave her face a yellow cast.

"Ooh, you're getting fat," she told Berri, patting her bulging belly. "How far along?"

"Six weeks," Berri said, clutching the presents to her chest.

"We've been busy," Adele said, pointing at the chimney crawling crookedly up the side of the big brown house. Some of the bricks were chipped and discolored. "I laid them myself," she said proudly.

"You what?" Charlie asked.

"Laid them myself. What's wrong with that?"

"You could've hurt yourself, Mom."

"It's easier than you think. Chimney leans a bit to one side, but I don't think it's noticeable, do you?"

"No, Ma."

"Where?" Berri asked politely.

"Let's get inside before we turn into popsicles!"

They followed Adele up the back steps into the humid kitchen, and she ran her hand through her curly red wig, trailing a faint scent of synthetic hair. "What d'you think? Looks all right?"

Berri nodded.

"It doesn't look cheap or anything, does it?"

"You look like a million bucks, Ma," Charlie said, sounding exactly like his father.

"Yes, but what does Berri think?" Adele blinked at her.

The faint tension that had drifted in with them now stained the air between them. Berri could read irritation in Adele's posture.

"Very nice."

"I'm not convinced you're telling the truth, but thanks anyway. Coffee? Oh, let's have some wine."

"Excuse me a minute." Berri practically flew up the stairs, then paused in the hallway to catch her breath. The second floor was darker than the first, curtains drawn, mothball odors emanating from the hallway closets. She composed herself in the bathroom and gazed at her reflection in the mirror, startled by her tense expression, lines pulling the skin in all directions.

Mickie called to her from the bedroom. "Is that my son?"

"No, it's Berri." She stood in the doorway.

"Beautiful as always," he said.

Charlie came in behind her. "Hiya, Pop."

"So you're gonna make me a Grandpa?"

They spoke for a while, and then Berri went downstairs to join Adele, who handed her a wine glass.

"I can't have alcohol."

"I know. Charlie told me. That's mineral water."

"Thanks."

"Let's sit in the living room. Just us girls."

A black kitten was playing with tinsel beneath a Christmas tree mummified in angel hair and popcorn strings. Dishes of rainbow candy were scattered about the room.

Adele picked up the kitten and held him at an angle across her chest. He dug in his claws, terrified. "Stop! This is a brand new dress." She let the kitten go, and he scrambled for safety behind Berri's chair.

"So what's new, stranger?" Adele asked. Since when had they been close enough to jokingly call each other stranger?

"I'm healthy. Happy. I'm sure it's going to be a girl."

"Oh, how wonderful. Mickie'll be thrilled. Can't have enough granddaughters. Jimmy and the kids are coming over later, you know." Jimmy was Charlie's older brother, and his wife Ellen was Berri's chief ally at these gatherings. "There's something to be said for having kids early. Get it over with. That's what I did." Adele clapped her hands, finished with the whole mess.

"Is Mickie okay? He looks a little pale."

"Couldn't be better."

"But I thought the doctors . . . ?"

Adele waved her hand dismissively. "Oh, he's doing great."

Now the Accident Radio sputtered in a corner of the room, and

Adele's smile grew forced, cheeks wrinkling beneath the rouge. "That night," she said, "I got a call from the hospital. The nurse said, 'Mrs. Smith? Your husband's had a heart attack.' Just like that."

She didn't seem to notice the kitten pawing the rug near her feet. On the tree, tiny multicolored lights blinked on and off, making the angel's hair sparkle.

"Now Mickie wants to buy an RV. Go camping. And here goes, he wants a Nissan. Can you believe it? We've always bought American; now he wants a foreign car. Where's his loyalty?" She shivered. "Come here, I want to show you something."

Berri put her glass down and followed Adele into the hallway, where she swung open the closet door. "Look. Pictures." She reached behind the boots, pulled out a shoe box. She sorted through the photographs, then held one out to Berri. "I remember this. North of town. Two-family house. Little boy died. What a tragedy. Smoke inhalation." She handed Berri the stack, and in each photograph, flames reached for a blackened sky.

"Who took these?"

"I did. I used to go out with him, early on . . . . before he volunteered. People like us were called 'sparkers.' We'd drive out, watch the fire, take pictures. We got some good ones."

Now the kitten was purring against Adele's ankles.

"One time, they had a broken tower ladder, and Mickie helped rescue these two little girls with the cherry picker. He came home filthy, his face all sooty with just a little white showing around the eyes." Adele snatched the pictures back and put them in the shoe box. "You know, Berri, I won't bother you two after Mickie dies."

Berri tried to hide her surprise. "You're never a bother, Adele."

"I can be a real pain in the kazola sometimes."

Berri gave a tight-lipped smile.

"My mother used to drive Mickie crazy, and I'm just like her. Listen," she said, leaning forward conspiratorially, "take these pictures. I don't want Mickie to find them. He's been snooping around the house lately. I don't want him to be reminded."

"Charlie could put them in the attic for you."

"Take them," she said, pressing the box into Berri's hands. "Take the Accident Radio, too. I don't want to be reminded."

"All right."

"They're scary pictures, don't you think?"

"Yes, Adele, they are."

Just then the radio emitted a flurry of static, and a loud voice announced a three-alarm down by the pier. Almost at once, they heard a commotion upstairs—a thump on the ceiling, raised voices.

"What's going on up there?" Adele hollered.

Mickie came tromping down the stairs with Charlie stumbling after him.

"He wants to go," Charlie said, "I keep telling him he can't . . . "

"Nobody's gonna tell me anything," Mickie said, buttoning his shirt, zipping his fly. "I've been lying in that frackin' bed long enough."

"Mickie," Adele said, her eyes growing suddenly huge.

He froze her with a look. "You can't stop me."

At the bottom of the stairs, he whipped open the closet and pulled out a black canvas coat with phosphorescent yellow tape stuck to the arms, a beat-up helmet with number 311 on its frontpiece and a pair of caked, black rubber boots. He quickly snapped the fasteners shut.

"Mom . . . ." Charlie had a stricken look. "Do something."

"No," she said, "let him go if he wants. Let him be a Big Hero."

"That's right." Mickie grabbed a pair of gloves by the stove and charged out the back door.

"Mom!" Charlie pleaded with her.

"Let him go."

They all stood by the kitchen window as Mickie got into his Mustang and stuck a red strobing beacon on the car roof, their faces caught in its flickering glare.

"He'll be gone for an hour, maybe two," Adele said calmly. "I'll put his lunch away."

✳

"Hey, Grannie, watch this!" Six-year-old Tina tore in from the hallway, cartwheeling over the living room rug and landing in a heap at Adele's feet, the idea of a second Christmas jerking at her limbs like puppet strings.

"These kids," Adele shook her head, "they let them run wild."

"I'm right here, Mom," Ellen said from the sofa.

Adele sniffed. The Accident Radio was silent for once, volume turned down. "I wonder where the boys are."

"In the attic, playing with the trains." Ellen stood and stretched. She had an auburn bob and sturdy legs beneath cinnamon-colored support hose. "I need a real cup of coffee, not this decaf dreck. Berri?"

In the kitchen, Ellen checked on the turkey, picking tiny pieces off the breastbone and tossing them to the kitten. "Get a load of Adele's wig, huh?" Ellen laughed. Then she lowered her voice to a fierce whisper. "Christmas was the pits. You guys're lucky you missed it. Mickie and Adele fought the whole time. We tried to get them to go out for a drive, but Adele wouldn't budge. She has to punish everybody."

Tina came running into the kitchen, whacking at her pink dress with open palms. "Gramma says I'm not a boy because my pee-pee fell off!"

"Huh?" Ellen's jaw dropped.

"She says she used the powder puff in the bathroom on me when I was a baby, and my pee-pee fell off. That's how come I'm a girl!"

Ellen pointed at the living room. "You march in there and tell Grandma you know all about penises and vaginas!"

Tina stomped her tiny foot. "She says she put the powder puff on her pee-pee, and hers fell off, too!"

"Oh, that's just great." Ellen turned to Berri, her whisper intensifying. "She has to be the most aggravating woman in the world. She never offers to take care of the kids; I have to practically force them on her. All she wants is for them to be still. And tell me, does she actually know what her sons do for a living? Does she even have a clue?"

Now turning and facing the living room, Ellen cupped her hands over her mouth. "Vaginas and penises!" she yelled.

Tina tentatively touched Berri's silver earring. "I'm getting my ears pierced when I grow up."

"Berri!" Adele hollered back. "Go upstairs and see what those boys are up to!"

✳

The attic stairs were narrow and slippery, the doorway deceptively short. Berri narrowly missed bumping her head. "Hey, you guys," she said. Charlie and his older brother Jimmy and Jimmy's son, Jason, were all bent over the electric train set. "Your mother wants to see you."

Charlie gave her one of his sighs, and Jimmy crossed his arms. They looked alike from a distance, except that Jimmy was going gray.

"Coming?" she asked, not wanting to go back downstairs without them.

Jimmy turned to Charlie. "Y'know, your mother didn't even have the decency to take care of Jason when Tina was born. Ellen's parents volunteered. Butch and Liv must spend about ninety percent more time with their grandchildren than your mother does."

"She didn't move a muscle to stop him," Charlie said. "She told me, 'Let him go.'"

Jimmy watched the train zipping around the track. "It's the way she never gets off the subject of herself that's so fucking bothersome."

"Are you guys coming?" Berri insisted, but met with their passive resistance.

"In a minute," they said in unison. Like twins.

✳

By the time Berri got back downstairs, Ellen and Tina were outdoors throwing snowballs. Charlie, Jimmy and Jason had decided to stay in the attic awhile longer, so Berri found herself alone once again with Adele.

"We've got to stop meeting like this," Adele laughed.

"They'll be down in a second."

"Well," she said, ears turning pink. "Mickie and I always kid around. I call him dummy, he calls me she-devil. But we love each other."

The kitten was chasing invisible bugs across the rug.

Now she moved closer, her voice growing soft as a snowflake. "When I was Tina's age," she confessed, "they came and took our house. Just took it away. Called us Japs."

The phone rang, and Berri's heart jumped, but Adele ignored it, smoothing the lap of her cranberry-colored dress. "I lost my bike," she continued. "My mother had to sell her tea set. The furniture went, everything." She clutched the string of pearls at her throat. "You learn to hold on to what little you've got. You learn to cling . . . ."

The phone kept ringing, and Berri couldn't stand it anymore. She got up from her chair, but Adele grabbed her wrist. Her fingers were cold.

"You know, Berri, I'm as American as apple pie." Eyes glistening, Adele tightened her grip. "But I've learned that sometimes . . . . you've just got to let go."

"I know," Berri said, feeling each ring in some new part of her body. "I know."

Messages

The cancer started in the epithelium of the woman's neck and sank like a crab in the murk where it took root and grew out of control until, one day, she could feel the lump with her fingers, and she shivered, knees stiffening; she pulled her hand away and then once again reached up to feel the walnut-sized lump at the back of her neck. And she knew before they performed the biopsy what it was, and the doctors didn't have to tell her—her, a registered nurse—that the tumor, wrapped around important nerves and blood vessels, was inoperable, and that she, Julia Kotter, had less than six months to live.

✳

Grover Lee tilted his red face closer and rested his oiled muscular arms on her shoulders, accidentally grazing the joystick with his elbow; his wheelchair's electrical hum and click startled her as the narrow rubber wheels rolled toward her feet, and she cried out as if she were a lost child, all the lights on in all the buildings but nothing reminding her of home. And Grover Lee said, "You're not going to die. I won't let you," his scarred face puckering like a drying sponge. His narrow, upturned eyes were the color of dried peas and his brown mustache always smelled slightly of string cheese. He had recurrent nightmares about being buried alive under a mound of dead bodies, the corpse above him pushing down hard, harder, trying to fuck him up the ass; that was Vietnam, he told her. That was the U.S. Army. "Leave your husband and come live with me," he said.

＊

"You've got to put up a fight," Ed Kotter told his wife, and she said, "You're just a real estate agent. What would you know about cancer?" She was skinny and pale, had weepy blonde hair and small irregularly shaped teeth, her green eyes retreating far back in her skull as if all those years at the V.A. hospital had made her reluctant to see things more clearly. And now she had another bad nose bleed and was pressing one of the linen handkerchiefs to her face.

With a sigh, Ed sat down on the bed beside her, knowing how much she hated his optimism, his drive to succeed, the methodical way he conducted his life. "One thing they say about cancer is . . . . the patients who fight live longer."

"I've seen depressed patients walk right out of the hospital, and I've seen the most optimistic people in the world die agonizing deaths. So don't tell me what to do, Ed."

"I won't let you give up." He ran his cigarette fingers over the pearly white buttons of her blouse, circling a spot of blood twice as if he could somehow protect her.

＊

Sadie ran home from school every day to be with her mother. She sat on the edge of the springy bed and held her mother's hand, fetched her things, switched stations on the TV. As the weeks passed, her mother's face grew sharper, more defined, the lines of her smile settling parenthetically into the waxy skin.

Late at night, Sadie overheard her parents' long, hushed conversations in the next room, their words swirling above her head like disturbed dust motes. Something in her father's tone frightened her, and she couldn't sleep, thrashing and sweating until her sheets were soaked, and she ended up curled on the floor by the foot of the bed, listening to the mechanical hum of the house.

One day, Sadie ran upstairs to an empty room. Her mother's bed was freshly made, the windows thrown wide open. A warm

California breeze lifted her wispy brown bangs and sent her skirt nuzzling between her legs. "Mom?"

Down the hall, her father stood in front of the bathroom mirror, a soft green light muting his usually robust face. As he watched her through the mirror, his eyes glittered, a fierceness burning inside. His hands were fisted into tight white knobs, the fingers hidden from her as if they'd been sliced off.

"Dad, where's Mom?"

"She's dead, Sadie," he said in a voice stretched as taut as the wiry lines of his face. His chin jutted outward, pointing at her. "She died today, while you were at school."

"But she couldn't've died!" Sadie cried. "She's got three more months at least. She told me so. She can't die yet!"

And her father gazed at her dumbly, his body strangely erect. He didn't go to her or even open his arms, he just stood in the green-lit bathroom, watching her with his marble gaze. And Sadie ran into her room and locked the door and thrashed around in the settled dust, knocking old toys off their shelves, hurling school books at the floral-patterned wallpaper.

∗

Grover Lee's sister Zippora drove him to the funeral, and all through the service he sat shivering with grief. He bit his lips, dug his nails into the wheelchair arms' vinyl padding, couldn't prevent the tears from funnelling down the crevices of his face.

At the wake, he spoke briefly with Ed, wondering how much he knew, realizing he knew nothing. Ed Kotter wore a salesman's smile, but his eyes had the bleary look of an accident victim's, swollen from inside like those dime-store plastic fish bags, the irises two goldfish swimming around, aimless and trapped.

Grover Lee wheeled up to the coffin and stared at Julia's body a long time, wishing he were dead, too. He wanted to be laid out beside her; they'd share the coffin like a foxhole, open wide their cotton eyes and reach for each other with stiffened arms. They'd press their dry lips together, and their kiss would be magical; they'd instantly crumble to dust, a dust so fine, the powder would rise up billowing in the air.

*

Sadie's best friend at school, Elise, explained that cancer sometimes jumped from mother to daughter like a hungry flea. Elise knew because her father was a research scientist at UCLA, and she read all his journals. Sadie began feeling for lumps in the bathroom stalls at school, running her fingers over her breasts, probing her neck and abdomen. She found cuts and scabs she never knew existed, discovered the exact shape of her knuckles, watched her pupils dilate and contract in the spotted mirror above the sink.

In class, she tried to concentrate, but everything her teachers said blew out the window like so much chalk dust. She remembered the walker her mother had used, how the metal had grown dull with grease from her hands; she remembered how thin her mother was, as if someone had punched holes in the bottoms of her feet and all the life had just seeped out. The bad smell that came from her mouth, as if the cancer were lurking right behind her tongue, a dead thick clump of cells. The pills on her bedside table and the glasses of tepid tap water that left white rings on the dark varnish.

At night, her father draped his gray jacket over a kitchen chair and rolled up his shirt sleeves and made dinner, his face stamped with the same smile he'd worn all day. He asked her about school in a voice that wasn't interested.

And sometimes, after dinner, he hunted through her mother's bureau drawers, drawers full of underwear and cardigan sweaters and rolled-up knee socks, but never seemed to find what he was looking for. He paced the kitchen floor in his Hush Puppies, or else marched up and down the stairs, mumbling to himself like a crazy person.

They never spoke about her mother, even though Sadie wanted to, longed to. She had bad dreams, dreamt she got cancer of the neck, of the ovaries, had black rotting holes in her stomach; she dreamt spoons and forks twisted all by themselves around her fingers, fork tongs digging deep into her flesh.

✳

Ed's daughter frightened him: the way she looked at him, always expecting more, something better. He hated the careless way she walked, tripping over her feet and bumping into doorways, hated the brutal, mindless way she plucked the hair from her face, scraping her skin with hangnailed fingers, hated the way she sucked on her lower lip, and the way her eyes welled predictably at night as they watched TV together. During the commercial breaks, he peeked at her—legs tucked underneath her skirt, hands twisted awkwardly in her lap, face calm and shiny, almost feverish, her glassy eyes reflecting miniature images from the TV screen.

Ever since his wife's death, Ed's thoughts had begun to frighten him—bizarre sexual fantasies involving the new cleaning lady, and an obsession with death—his own and everyone else's. He contemplated his wife's suicide over and over until he watched it like a movie in his mind's eye, taking his own life with her every single night in his dreams.

Watching television helped Ed forget, and so all during that long warm winter, he watched sports and prime-time sitcoms, wildlife specials, the news. He bought himself things—a brand-new stereo and CD player, a computer he never used, an expensive watch and a bunch of red ties, handsome tailored shirts he stacked unopened on the closet shelves.

Obsessively, he searched through Julia's belongings, hoping to find a note that would explain it all, but there was nothing. He had very little to say to his daughter; they hardly ever spoke, and the sight of her sometimes filled him with guilt, and for that he almost hated her.

✳

Jan went to work for the Kotters in early March, and there was so much to do. The kitchen was full of baked-on grease, the bathroom was mildewed, dust coated every surface of the house like the powdery crust of a moonscape. Jan was thin and blonde, hardworking, a chain smoker. During the evenings, Ed trailed around after her with a large glass ashtray, begging her to quit smoking as if his life depended on it. He tucked pamphlets from the American Cancer Society into her purse along with her weekly paycheck.

He was short but dignified-looking with spiky gray hair and a trim gray mustache, and it was the mustache that killed her. From the first, she'd felt an instant, undeniable chemistry between them, a chemistry that made them cautious, uncertain, almost shy around each other. He watched from a distance as she scrubbed the kitchen floor, and she sensed that he liked the way her small breasts clapped together over the wet linoleum.

Wednesday evening, she came upon him accidentally in the master bedroom, shaking one of his dead wife's shoes as if he were trying to dislodge a pebble.

"I'll come back later," she said, but he raised his hand to stop her.

"Jan," he said, "if you ever find a note, a crumpled piece of paper, even an envelope . . . . don't throw it away. Give it to me."

"Of course," she said, unable to ignore the alarming erection pushing against his eggshell-colored trousers.

Then he did something strange; he hurled the high-heeled shoe at the wall and mashed his fist to his mouth, bending his head as if he'd given up hope. "Please don't go," he murmured through his fist, and Jan put down her feather duster. She sat on the edge of his dead wife's bed and started to unbutton her workshirt—a powder blue cotton blouse with JAN sown over the breast pocket in heavy navy thread.

✳

During the afternoons, while her father was out selling movie star's mansions to entertainment lawyers and Japanese businessmen, Sadie locked herself in her bedroom and lay naked on her bed, imagining herself dead, her soul ascending from her body and hovering just inches from the cracked ceiling, or else skittering along like a helium balloon caught in a household current. She wanted to feel dead, dream dead, wanted desperately to peel away the layers of being alive and get at the very core of death, rising, plateauing out, rising again. But always, there was the ceiling, the limit to her imagination, her own nakedness bringing her back to life.

Sadie ran her hands over her skin, feeling for the lumps she knew were there—the mutating cells, the knots, hidden lesions. Touching herself roughly, she thought about the boys at school—how they teased her, made fun of her name, poked her in the chest and put tacks on her chair, how they tugged at her long brown hair, faces flushed, their fingers cold against her skin. They plucked at her arm as if she might burn them alive. And her face heated and her mind went blank, and she knew, someday soon, she'd crash through the ceiling.

✳

"You don't know who I am," whispered Jan. "You never ask me anything about myself. I could be a bank robber, for all you cared."

They were lying on the bedroom floor on the soft, thick carpet. Jan was naked to the waist and Ed was kneading her flesh with his small neat hands.

"You especially don't like me to talk when we make love," she said. "It's like you want to pretend I'm somebody else. I know who you're thinking of. I know how much I look like her, I've seen pictures."

"Don't be ridiculous," he said too quickly, needing her remarkable resemblance to his dead wife—the flatness of her stretched body, the blonde-dishrag hair, the wanness of her small stare. Each of her breasts fit almost entirely into his mouth, and his hands knew the curved wonder of her ass; she was tight and deep and brought him oblivion.

It was true that he never thought about Jan's private life, never thought about her at all outside the context of their afternoons together—her rough Ajax-smelling hands, her facial skin flecked with

Tide, her work clothes smeared with dirt from the greasiest corners of his house. She breathed a steady rhythm as she worked, calming him, and her body flattened out, widened like a flooded river as they made love, and he often imagined he could mold her into something different.

"Let me talk," she pleaded, closing her eyes as he slipped into her, and, smoothing her pale brow with his fingertips, he whispered, "Shhhh."

Grover Lee burned for Julia, ached for her, obsessively resurrected her in his mind—her nimble fingers buttoning her nurse's uniform, the lipstick stains she left on Styrofoam cups. He spent hours conjuring her up. The linen closet where they first met was as big as a bathroom, light on bright above them. He followed her in, shut the door; and how she trembled, thin as a bird, her thin arms, thin legs; and the hunger on her face as she knelt and pressed her open mouth to his belt buckle, turquoise oval set in silver, her breath pouring hot as boiled liquid through his clothes; and his love for her flooding the linen closet, burning brighter than the harsh 80-watt bulb that sent long shadows sliding down their faces; and the way she clawed at his zipper—but then she stopped, staring at the stumps that ended his big thighs so abruptly; and how in gentle wonder she unpinned the shortened pants' legs, opened them up, rolled them back, and gazed in amazement at the healed-over stumps, shiny pink as baby doll heads; and how, oh God how she rested her soft moist hands on them and shut her eyes, the better to feel their new-toy contact; and God, oh God how he loved her.

✳

In June, a boy named Buck asked Sadie to a party. Four couples sat around the Malibu basement, drinking Cokes mixed with rum. The boys made sweaty, dirty jokes; they seemed small to her, girlish and agitated. Buck could hardly sit still; he did cartwheels over the basement floor, then held her around the waist and breathed on her damp neck. He had red lips and pink cheeks flushed from doing backflips. She liked his eyes because they reminded her of a movie star's, and she let him kiss her.

Buck's brother, Arnie, and a girl named Gail were making out on a yellow beanbag chair in the corner. Buck pulled Sadie onto the sofa with him, slipping a blanket over them, and they held each other lightly. Sadie, drunk, ran her fingernail over his zipper, liking the sound it made, click-click-click. She took the metal tab and pulled, and suddenly he was hot all over her, smelling of car oil and corners of earth and blueberry popsicles, his wet tongue in her ear, now lapping at her front teeth.

Buck took Sadie's T-shirt off and, dipping underneath the blanket, kissed her breasts. She gazed in amazement at the round bump of his head, became hypnotized, pulled along, dragged under. Now Buck's brother had his clothes off, his sunburned back and soft white cheeks exposed to her, and the beanbag chair made a whooshing sound as the couple jerked back and forth.

Buck lay hot and smeared across her, pushed himself into her, and Sadie met his nervous rollings with a few slow twists of her own, as if she'd done this all her life.

And afterward they passed around a joint and, lit by the blue television light, watched old M*A*S*H episodes back-to-back.

✳

Sadie's father was sitting on the bedroom floor, sorting through a cardboard box of her mother's letters and notes. Her mother used to leave messages all over the house—reminder notes, silly doodles, Valentine cards with hearts and X's dragging along the bottom. Julia believed in recycling and saved bits of string and Christmas wrapping, ads that came with the utility bills. She picked things out of the trash other people had thrown away.

"Damn!" he said, tossing a piece of paper behind him on the rug, where it bounced once and rolled under the bed. He thumped the cardboard box against the floor.

"Dad?" she said softly. "I'm home."

And he looked as though he didn't know her, his gaze wandering clear through her. He'd lost all sense of who she was, and her heart jammed up against her ribs, and she wanted him to hold her now, right now! Right now, but he didn't move, he just leaned against the sturdy sides of the cardboard box and shut his eyes. And she slammed her bedroom door, hating him.

*

Buck told Sadie his parents were in Rio for the week, and they settled back against the sofa, sipping wine coolers. Then Arnie joined them in the basement, sinking into the beanbag chair across the way. "This is an antique," he said, patting the yellow plastic. He had short curly blonde hair and long jeans-covered legs that stuck out over the sides like sprawling blue leaves.

During a Toyota commercial, Arnie stood up and took his shirt off. His chest was skinny and hairless. Then, as if on cue, Buck stood up, too, and took off his shirt, and they both sat down beside her, the sofa sinking with their weight. She could feel their heat and the fluttering of their breath, and she froze, staring dumbly at the set.

The Monkees were prancing around in the desert, jumping up and disappearing, then suddenly reappearing on the ground. Buck slipped his arm over her shoulder, kissed her lightly on the lips; then Arnie put his hand on her knee and ran it slowly up her thigh. Her breath came out quick and irregular as the two brothers peeled her out of her clothes. Suddenly, the three of them were tumbling naked over the hard carpeted floor, Buck whispering, "It's all right; it's all right," in her ear. And Sadie wanted to run, wanted to scream or cry out, but she felt herself being sucked into them like a tiny fish into the undulating heart of a squid, the way they held her, fed off her. And Arnie, standing, made her kneel on the floor and take him into her mouth. She did exactly what he said, afraid to do anything else; they were two strong boys. Buck scrambled around and entered her from behind, and the two brothers stroked her like some sick animal they'd found. Her knees scoured the prickly carpet as they rocked her back and forth between them, moaning low. She was the place their cocks met in the middle of, crushing her heart.

The brothers hammered into her until she buckled, until she felt packed as compressed steel; when they came, their cries rising like the hunger of birds, Sadie almost blacked out, became a blankness they filled with their will, a blank page they smeared all their longing on.

✳

Grover Lee had to tell someone before he burst. It was like the time in the jungle when he'd seen the ruby-colored bird, its beauty knocking him out, obliterating the war and everything else while it sang its sweet, warbling song. He had to tell someone, and so he'd gone back to the base to fetch his buddy, A.J., and they'd squatted in the bush for over an hour, listening.

Now Grover Lee had to tell someone, so he did a stupid thing. He picked up the phone and dialed Julia's number.

"Hello?" Ed Kotter answered.

"I loved her too, y'know."

After he hung up, he felt terrible, as if he'd just shot another gook simply because he couldn't tell which side the guy was on.

✳

Rolling herself up in a green wool blanket, Sadie wondered what her mother looked like right now. Was she really a rotting corpse, withered as dried fruit, fungus-black, her skin a leathery pouch filled with powdered blood? Was her hair still pinned to her head the way the mortician had done it, or did it spill over the coffin lining like chicken soup funnelling down a sink drain? Were her hands folded over her chest, the last X she'd ever scrawl? Had her pink dress sunken on her body like the stale, cracked icing on an old birthday cake?

Sadie wanted to know, wanted to dig up the coffin and jump inside, rub herself against whatever was left. Wanted to inhale the coffin's closed air and know what death smelled like. At the very least, she wanted to lie on the ground where her mother was buried and press her face to the prickly grass, wrap her arms around the tombstone and clutch at the meaning of the words carved there.

Sadie missed her mother, missed her mother, missed her.

So far, they'd been to the cemetery twice, laying pink carnations on the grave, pink being her mother's favorite color.

✳

The man spoke urgently. "I loved her too, y'know." Then the line went dead, but the implication crashed into Ed's consciousness like a tree limb through glass. He glared at the phone as if it had bitten him.

Turning on his heels, he tromped upstairs to his daughter's room and hesitated for a moment in the doorway, eyes slowly adjusting to the darkness. Sadie was lying on her bed, gazing vacantly at the ceiling.

"Sadie, I've got something to tell you," he said, deciding to spit out the secret that'd been poisoning him for months. "Your mother didn't actually die of cancer. She committed suicide. She took an overdose of pills."

His daughter said nothing, just kept staring at the ceiling.

He stepped into the room. "I should've told you sooner. Sadie, did you hear what I said?" And he would force her to look at him, to recognize his pain just as she recognized her own; he would aim the truth like a gun between those darkly glittering eyes. "Sadie," he said firmly. "Look at me."

And suddenly, she turned her head, her gaze fixing him like points of light from glass shards, and this child's face, filled with hatred, shocked him.

"Sadie," he said, "your mother didn't leave you any kind of note, did she? Did she say anything about a man?"

And her gaze sank needles into the liquid tissue of his eyes.

✳

Her father's face hovered above her, light blue veins pumping beneath the skin of his temples, and he asked, "Sadie, was there any note?"

Turning away, she lay stiff and knotted as old rope, refusing to answer. She remembered the jars on her mother's bedside table—five bottles holding multicolored pills, some big, some tiny, some oblong, some round.

"Sadie?"

In a far corner of the room, a pink spider was building its transparent web.

"Sadie, please don't do this to me." Suddenly, her father's face broke over her like busted plaster, his sobs penetrating through to her bone. Tears smeared his face and long clear strings hung from his nose, bubbles forming in the corners of his mouth as he spoke. "Sadie, I'm sorry! I should've told you sooner, I just didn't have it in me . . . ."

And from the darkness of the room came her mother's arms, cool and perfumed; they surrounded her, scooped her up, and she was warmed by her mother's breath, which was no breath at all but a mild breeze coming through her open window.

"Sadie," her father whispered.

And she wanted to laugh, because he didn't understand. Because her mother was right there with them in the room. She took a deep breath, and the breath turned convulsive, great sobs shaking her frame. Her father held her while she sobbed, and she wanted to tell him, yes, there was a note, there was! But she couldn't get the words out.

The day before her mother died, she ran her hand gently through Sadie's hair and wrote a word on her chest, a private game of theirs. "Love," said the word. Then with two strokes, her mother drew an X across her mouth and blew the kiss over.

And Sadie, smiling, caught it in her hand.

Corporation Beach

Cassius lay on the sofa with his head hanging over the side. He liked to pretend he could walk across the ceiling. His brother didn't know it, but he was upside-down. Rollo had a blonde butch cut and the longest, whitest eyelashes anybody'd ever seen. Cassius held his hand in front of his eyes and squeezed his fingers together, trying to pinch Rollo's head off, but it didn't do any good. He was still hanging there, his upside-down frown turned into a weird kind of smile.

"Ma! Hurry up!" They were waiting for their mother to take them to the beach. Birdie Gold was late as usual, stooping five times over her makeup mirror to check her lipstick, glancing around the room as if the furniture might get up and walk away the minute her back was turned.

This summer, they were renting the top part of a house on Corporation Beach. Downstairs was the concession stand, where Mrs. Monroe came every morning to grill hotdogs and whip milkshakes. She was skinny and had long dark hair and a stern expression that told you she was busy and couldn't be disturbed. At first Cassius was afraid of her. She would stand over the grill and bite her lips, pale face steaming. But then one day she gave him a candy bar, and he decided that he liked her after all.

She had two daughters and a baby boy who played with them in the back yard. They'd go down to the basement and show each other their bare bottoms, or else hunt for rabbits and snakes in the dunes. Since they were living above a concession stand, they'd gotten the place Dirt Cheap, Cassius's father said. But early mornings, before Mrs. Monroe came, it almost felt like a real home.

Now Cassius's mother came out of her bedroom and handed them the beach umbrella, and Rollo dragged it down the stairs, whacking the wooden steps with its handle.

"Pick it up!" Birdie Gold was the exact opposite of Mrs. Monroe—short and plump, with shoulder-length blonde hair she pinned up every night. The bobby pins fit like a bathing cap of X's on her head, and their father always teased her, calling her his little pinhead. She wore pink lipstick and blue eye shadow, and her favorite food was shrimp. She cooked the shrimps in boiling water on the stove, smelling up the whole top floor, then let them cool in the refrigerator. She carried them in a wax paper bag to the beach, where she sat on the old wool blanket his father had saved from the Army. Then she dipped the shrimps in ketchup and yelled at the boys not to swim out too far.

Downstairs, Flo and Penny Monroe and their baby brother, Jared, waited by the back door. As soon as Cassius saw Flo, his heart did a flip in his chest. Just last week, she'd shown them her bum, lifting the blue-flowered dress and pulling her pink panties down, then yanking them back up almost too quick for anyone to see. She was exactly his age, seven. Penny was nine and wore glasses and stood with one hand on her hip, as if she wanted to be someplace else.

Jared's teeth were like glistening white barnacles. He had sandy-blonde hair and his bare little chest was brown from the sun. He wore crinkly rubber pants over his diapers and said, "Gaahhh!" poking the end of a blue comb in his mouth. Penny got the combs from the concession stand. She let Jared play with them, and he'd spend the morning sticking them in his mouth or down his pants; then she'd put them back in the concession stand display box. They came in all colors—blue and red and pink and green and tangerine.

"Hail, hail, the gang's all here!" said his mother, tromping down the stairs. "Howdy doody, Iris!" she hollered out front to Mrs. Monroe. "Cool your jets awhile, kiddies."

The Monroe girls were leaning against the tall cardboard boxes in the front hallway—boxes holding huge tins of ketchup, enormous bottles of pickles and relish, cartons of Good 'n Plenties and Charleston Chews. They stared at Cassius and Rollo with their big, unblinking blue eyes. All the Monroes had blue eyes.

"Your horse head's ready," Penny said. "Daddy took it out of the kiln yesterday, and it didn't have a single crack." Their father was a potter in Brewster.

"Sometimes they have cracks." Flo's eyes widened. "But yours came out perfect!"

"Well, not exactly *perfect*," Penny said, sneering at Rollo, who was hopping from foot to foot in front of her. Rollo was always trying to get Penny's attention. When he pulled down his pants that time, he turned around and wiggled his peter at them, and Penny screamed, and after that they stopped playing games in the basement.

Being with Flo always made Cassius feel peculiar, as if his stomach were melting. She had long dark hair and shiny blue eyes that seemed to see right through him, as if she knew his secrets. She was tough as a boy and liked playing rough games, the rougher the better. When Cassius was It, he'd chase after her until he tagged her, and they'd knock each other down and tumble in the dirt, and a ferociousness would come over him, and he'd want to hurt her, make her cry, because she never seemed to notice him the way he wanted her to. And if only he could tag her really hard and make her cry, then maybe she'd notice him. Except that Flo never cried; or else, if she did, she hid it so well you couldn't tell.

After the mothers were finished talking, Mrs. Gold led them down the winding path toward the beach parking lot, while Rollo dragged the umbrella, making a snail's trail in the dirt.

"Our dad made us cups and plates of our very own," Penny said, pushing her glasses back up her nose.

"Our dad bought us Patriots T-shirts." Rollo grinned at her, showing off his big, gappy white teeth. "Our dad lets us stay up late to watch Ed Sullivan!"

"Where's he work, anyway?"

"He's a film distributor in Boston."

"A film distributor?" Penny said, as if she'd never heard anything so stupid in her life. "What's a film distributor?"

"He mails movies to the different theaters," Cassius explained, scraping his toes in the dirt.

"What d'you mean? You mean he's a mailman?" Flo asked, and Cassius blushed. He didn't want her thinking his father was a mailman.

"Not a mailman, nerfo!" Rollo laughed. "A film distributor!"

Penny rolled her eyes and hurried away, as if she suddenly couldn't stand them anymore. She caught up with Cassius's mother and started talking in a very grown-up voice. The sky was the color of a blue balloon blown to the breaking point. In front of them, a little girl dragged a bag of buttered popcorn across the sand, spilling kernels which the sea gulls spotted. The sand, mixed with mica, shone like Christmas sparkle. Flo squatted and scooped up a handful, and Cassius copied her, feeling the grains like hot liquid shivering through his fingers.

Straight ahead was the jetty, where the big gray rocks tumbled into the water. Sea gulls standing on the highest rocks looked stuffed. Whenever his father came down for the weekend, he'd take the boys with him to the very end of the jetty and say, "This is the life, guys!" If he'd been drinking, he'd lose his balance and swing his arms, almost tipping over, long toes gripping the wet rocks. "You boys've got it made in the shade," he'd say.

Now Rollo dropped the umbrella in the sand. "Can we play in the rowboat, Ma?"

"Just be careful." Cassius's mother spread the Army blanket on the sand and started smoothing suntan lotion over her arms and legs, making sure she covered every spot. Whenever his mother sat on the beach, she read mystery books or else knitted sweaters for the wintertime. She wore the blackest sunglasses and a sun hat made of straw that tied with a silky swatch of cloth under her chin. She never wore a bathing suit, just loose-fitting shorts and sleeveless blouses—calico, or pink or white, the collar unbuttoned so she could get a little sun on her chest. She'd gotten so fat, she told them, she couldn't fit into her swimsuit anymore. Her thighs were white and doughy, little green bruises and a rivery blue vein coloring the skin like markings on a faded board game. Their father liked to pinch her roundest places and make her squeal.

The old abandoned rowboat had been dragged up onto the shore of the cove. Penny and Flo sat in the bow, Rollo took the middle, and Cassius got stuck with the baby in back. Rollo gazed out over the water, his bony hands clasping the sides of the boat. "Hey, Penny!" he said. "Wanna go out to the jetty with me?"

"No, thanks!" She made a sour face, then leaned to one side, slightly tipping the boat. "Haul anchor!"

"Aye, aye, Cap'n!" Rollo saluted her.

The two girls looked at each other and giggled, while Rollo rocked the boat. Cassius held onto the baby. "Cut it out!" he said, excited and scared at the same time. Rollo always went wild around Penny. He did whatever she told him to, no matter how stupid it was.

"Shhh!" Penny hissed. "It's coming around the corner!"

Flo cupped her hands over her mouth, her bright eyes narrowing, eyebrows wiggling under the soft brown bangs.

"You two talkin' dirty?" Rollo said.

A black beetle scuttled across the sand. The sun came down like a red-hot on top of Cassius's head. There were holes in the bottom of the rowboat big as silver dollars, some as big as softballs. Cassius could see through to the wet sand.

The only dirty words Cassius knew were damn and hell. Whenever his father came home from work, he'd swear about his job. His mother would make them both a scotch on the rocks, and they'd sit in the living room while the boys played outside, or else watched TV in the den. While his parents drank, his father would talk and his mother would listen; his father would say what a mess it was out there, how everyone was out to get you, and his mother would nod and sip her drink. Damn this and damn that, his father would say, to hell with the whole damn world. Then it would be time for dinner.

Penny had a pug nose like a button on a beret. She was always teasing Cassius, but the worst part was when Flo went along. "Shh . . . . it's coming around the corner!" she hollered in his face. "Get it?!"

Cassius decided to ignore her. If he ignored her, then maybe she'd stop bothering him and bug somebody else instead. He gazed beyond the jetty at the far side of the beach where a turquoise truck was parked in the sand. Some men were hauling a huge black bag toward the truck. Men were always clearing away driftwood and burnt logs from the beach. Sometimes they rode their trucks so close to shore, sunbathers jumped up from the sand.

Cassius watched the men for a while, trying to make himself invisible. In order to become invisible, you had to concentrate really hard on something else. Sometimes it worked; sometimes it didn't. When Penny hollered, "He doesn't get it!" Cassius knew it wasn't working. He gave her a mean stare and told her to shut up.

"Look, he's blushing!" she screeched.

Jared took the blue comb out of his mouth and stuck it into his diaper. "Hah!" he said, patting the crinkly rubber pants. He flapped his chubby arms and a clean, powdered-baby smell rose up from him.

"Shh . . . . it's coming around the corner!" Flo's eyes flashed like lightning bugs. A breeze picked up her hair, flicking long strands of it across her face.

"He doesn't get it!" Penny gripped the sides of the chalky row-boat, working her skinny middle back and forth.

"I do so!"

"Get what?" Penny's eyes lit up. "Get what?"

"Shh! It's comin' around the corner!" Cassius said. Something was coming around the corner, maybe a monster, or else a ghost or something. He got it all right. He got it. His throat felt full of hot soup, and his eyes hurt from staring too hard at the million minia-ture suns glinting off the far waves.

"Aw, he doesn't know what it means." Rollo glanced over his shoulder at his brother and smirked, and at that instant, Cassius hated his guts. Rollo used to be so much nicer, explaining the way bikes worked and teaching him the alphabet, offering to play catch. But lately, it was as if they weren't brothers at all.

"Do so!" Cassius hooked his arm around Jared's soft middle as they wobbled in the stern, cheeks and lips joggling with each bump.

"Do so!"

"Do not!" Rollo rasped.

"Calm down, kiddies!" his mother hollered from far away, her face a pale dot under the shade of the umbrella.

Jared reached his hand down into his rubber pants and pushed the comb around. "Bloo!" he said.

Cassius's hands hurt from gripping the sides of the rowboat. His bottom was sore from bouncing around on the splintered seat. Worst of all, he felt ganged up on. He wished he could disappear into thin air, become like the Invisible Man. Then he'd run around pinching everybody's bottom, pulling on their hair, and they'd never know where to look next. He'd be everywhere, like the wind. Like spider mites. Staring straight at Penny, he said, "I see London, I see France, I see Penny's underpants!"

"Oooh, he's gettin' dirty," Rollo cackled.

Penny smiled, tilting her head sideways so that her dirty blonde hair curled over her cheek. "So what?" Then she caught Rollo staring and squeezed her legs shut.

"First comes love, then comes marriage, then comes Penny inna baby carriage!" Flo sang, glancing at Cassius with wet, excited eyes. "First comes love . . . ."

"Shut up, pipsqueak!" Penny pushed her sideways.

"No, you shut up," Cassius said, rocking the boat as hard as he could. "You shut up! You!"

Penny jerked her whole body, making the boat wobble and tip. The boat swung first one way, then the other, sand and pebbles crunching underneath. Flo shrieked. Rollo helped Penny by arching his skinny body, and the boat crunched and groaned, tipping at a dangerous angle. They were going over, Cassius could tell. They were leaning so far to the right, his heart rocked sideways in his chest, and he was suddenly tumbling out of the boat. Jared fell to the bottom in a squealing heap, and Rollo rocked himself out and sprawled across the sand. They were all screaming, and the boat righted itself with a thwunk, and then Cassius was gazing up at the sky, sea gulls slowly circling above him.

"Hey!" his mother called from very far away; then he heard

footsteps slapping the sand.

Beyond the jetty, the men were still loading the black bag onto the truck. They crawled over the sand like ants. A hermit crab scuttled by, and Rollo reached out and caught it. Then he leapt to his feet and tossed it in the boat, and Penny shouted, "Cut it out, dumbhead!"

Rollo bent over his brother and frowned. "Hey, Gaseous-Cassius. You okay?"

Suddenly, Cassius's mother was hovering over him, crying, "You all right, baby?" She helped him up from the sand. With gentle hands, she brushed off his legs and the back of his swim trunks. Her eyes were anxious and her breath came out all even-spaced and hot.

"Yup," Cassius murmured, burying his toes in the scrunchy sand. A tiny piece of gravel stuck to the skin of his ankle, but he didn't bend down to pick it off. He didn't even shake his foot. Instead, he just stood perfectly still, taking one long deep breath.

An orange trash barrel yards away threw the smell of fried clams and banana slush at them. Sea gulls were crying out from the sky. Cassius tried not to blink as his eyes filled with tears. His mother once told him tears were made of salt water, that about a million years ago their ancestors had crawled out of the sea.

"Don't cry!" His mother sounded alarmed. She threw her arms around him, which only made him feel worse. "It's just a stupid old game. You're okay, honey."

Jared and Flo scrambled up from the bottom of the boat, their two pairs of eyes watching him over the chalk-white side. They watched him while he cried like a baby. They blinked in unison.

"Cassius and me got drowned," Rollo said, laughing harshly, and Penny told him to shut up. He made a looping, embarrassed dance in the sand, hopping over sharp pieces of gravel, shouting, "Yipes! Yipes! Yipes!"

Cassius started to laugh. He was laughing and crying at the same time.

"Yipes! Yipes! Yipes!" Rollo made everyone laugh, even their mother, who wiped Cassius's cheeks with the tail of her white blouse.

The truck honked behind them, and they all turned to look. It roared by, spitting sand, and tied to the flatbed was an enormous whale. The whale's black tail flapped over the tailgate as the truck headed up the beach toward the parking lot. And suddenly, they were all chasing it as fast as they could.

※

In the parking lot, three shirtless men stood around the front fender of the pickup truck, sweat dripping from their arms in sparkling drops. They wore the tan pants of the beach patrollers.

An orange-haired man seemed to be in charge. He kept pointing at the whale, then scratching the back of his neck, leaving reddened circles on the sweaty skin.

The whale was tied to the back of the truck with gray, frazzled ropes. "It's still alive," Birdie said, amazed. A small crowd had gathered behind them, and Penny was holding Jared tightly in her arms.

"I know what kind that is," Rollo said, wiping his mouth with the back of his hand. "A baby pilot." He grinned at Penny, who stuck her tongue out. The orange-haired man circled the truck, tightening the ropes, while the whale rolled its tiny eyes.

"His skin's all cracked!" Cassius shouted.

"Quiet, jerko." Rollo punched his arm.

The orange-haired man climbed onto the hood of the truck and looked down at the top of the whale. "It got beached about half a mile up," he told the crowd, pointing toward the jetty. The side of the whale closest to them was torn, its hide scraped from being dragged across the rocks. The black skin was milky from being out in the sun too long. The whale was lying perfectly still and could have been dead, except for the tiny opening at the top of its head that made a sucking sound.

"Damn thing must weigh a ton," the man said.

"Put him back in the water!" Cassius cried, but the orange-haired man pretended not to hear. Somebody snickered behind them, and his mother shushed him, resting her hands on his shoulders. Her face under the brim of her sun hat was sickly pale, almost green. She once told him the story of Jonah, how the whale had swallowed Jonah whole, how he'd lived in the belly of the whale by floating on his raft. Cassius couldn't imagine anybody ever living inside this whale; it was about the size of their sofa back home. You'd have to curl yourself up into a ball, and there wouldn't be enough room to move your arms and legs.

The orange-haired man jumped off the truck and opened the door, then pulled out a rifle. "Stand back, folks."

Cassius ran up to the truck.

"Hey, watch it, young fellah!"

He scrambled onto the flatbed and touched the whale's hide, which was rough as sandpaper and sticky wet. When the whale rolled its tiny black eyes, looking directly at him, Cassius almost screamed. There was pain in the sharp wet glint, pain and suffering. He felt a shiver run all through him, tickling his fingers where he touched the whale's skin.

Somebody grabbed him around the middle, and he let out a scream. His mother was dragging him, kicking and hollering, back into the crowd.

"Leggo!" he said, smashing his fists against her, something he'd never done before. When she stood him firmly on the asphalt, his head felt swollen to twice its size. His heart was beating like a tom-tom, and his face was pounding hot. He was going to throw up right there in the parking lot. The crowd was buzzing all around him. His mother pinned his shoulders down, while Flo gazed at him with her wide blue eyes.

"You can't shoot him!" Cassius hollered, but the orange-haired man just smiled. Then he pointed his finger and pulled an imaginary trigger.

"That does it," his mother said. She grabbed Cassius's hand and dragged him toward the path. "C'mon, kids. We're leaving."

Cassius dug in his heels, trying to wrench his arm away, but she had him in a firm grip and wouldn't let go. None of the other kids were following.

"I said, come on!" Birdie snapped, and Rollo started hopping from one leg to the other.

Finally wrenching free, Cassius raced back to the truck and pushed his way through the crowd. The parking lot was jammed with cars, and the tar was hot beneath his feet. "Why'd you have to catch him? Why don't you put him back in the ocean?"

"'Cause he's beached," Rollo said, picking his nose.

Cassius wanted to smack his brother—knock him flat on his peanut-shaped skull. Rollo was three years older and four inches taller and thought he knew more, but he didn't know anything.

"Sometimes whales lose their sense of direction," his mother said, catching up. She spoke softly in his ear, bending close. Her voice, gentle and tickly as a spring leaf, frightened him. Her breath was like a cold finger on his cheek. The hairs on the back of his neck stood up. "Some people think whales get sick and have to swim ashore because they know they're dying. It's too late to save him, Cassius. C'mon, let's go home, honey."

His eyes filled with hot, stinging tears. He was sick of crying, sick to death, but he couldn't stop himself. Flo worked her teeth over her lower lip and gazed at him as if he were a snake in the grass. Or a rabbit.

"But his skin's all cracked," Cassius said. "He can't breathe!"

The orange-haired man climbed back on the roof of the cab, rifle in hand. "Move back, folks," he said, but nobody moved.

"Good God," his mother breathed. "He isn't going to shoot it right in front of us?"

Suddenly, the whale started flopping around on the truckbed, its tail whipping at the crowd. Everyone jumped back. The metal creaked and groaned, and the orange-haired man sprang to the asphalt like a cat. "Holy Cripes!"

"Yay!" Cassius clapped, while his mother pressed his shoulders, trying to make him stop. She once told him whales weren't fish at all, but mammals, and that they were smart as human beings. Maybe even smarter.

"I got an idea!" Cassius said. "Let's get our buckets and fill them with water and pour it on the whale."

"Dumb," Rollo murmured.

"You're not allowed," said Penny.

The man climbed back onto the hood on all fours like a spider. His work boots made the metal sigh. He balanced himself on the truck's shiny rooftop. Sun glinted off the metal, spiked off the windows, the chrome, the running lights, the silver hubcaps. The man steadied himself and, spreading his legs wide apart, took careful aim at the whale's head. When he shot, the blast rocked his shoulder back.

The whale lay very still. Cassius's lungs ached, as if the bullet had ricocheted off the truck and pierced his chest. They waited for something to happen, for the man to step down, but instead, he aimed the gun again and fired.

Flo's mouth went soft with amazement. Jared drooled on the asphalt, milky spit drying fast in the blistering sun. The whale started to rock the truck, making the mud flaps wobble. All the loose things in the cabin rattled and clicked, all the bolts and clamps and welded pieces strained and shivered. The whale shook the truck like it was a too-heavy blanket, like it was his aluminum-foil armor. He heaved ferociously, arching his spine, and a sickening smell rose up from him—the smell of rotten meat and sun-baked seaweed.

The orange-haired man tried to balance himself on the rooftop, his teeth biting the air. He aimed the gun and fired crookedly into the side of the whale, and the whale stopped moving. Nobody said a word. They just stood there, inhaling the whale's sickening smell.

"Come on, kids." His mother grabbed his hand, pulling him toward the path. "Kids!" she said sharply. "Let's go!"

Cassius didn't put up a fight this time; instead, he let her drag him toward the house, a queasiness growing inside him like the flu. His head pounded and his sides ached and his throat was hoarse, and nobody had done a thing to save the whale. Nobody.

"So how come it's not dead yet?" Penny asked.

"I don't know." His mother's grip was too tight. Cassius twisted her wrist, but she wouldn't let go. He wanted to tell her it was okay, that he wouldn't run back to the truck, but his mouth had gone dry.

"Some whales eat people," Rollo said, running to catch up. "I heard of these killer whales that bite whole boats in half."

"Whales don't eat people," Penny sneered.

"Why's the whale keep jumping around?" Flo jogged beside him, her head bobbing gently on her skinny neck. She was fast for a girl, and much braver than him. Whenever Mr. Monroe took them fishing, she wasn't afraid to slide the thick worms onto the ends of the fish hooks.

"Those are its death throes," his mother explained. "Its skull is probably too thick for those bullets to penetrate."

"Deafrows?"

"Death throes!" Rollo repeated. "Like it's fighting to live, but it's gonna die just the same."

Cassius felt awful, as if he'd seen something he wasn't supposed to, a part of the world not meant for him. He wondered if all death was like that. He wondered if, when his grandfather died, it'd taken so long. The whale's eyes rolled like marbles inside its skull. Cassius knew he'd never forget those eyes as long as he lived.

Cassius's mother finally let go, and he fell into step with Flo. Behind them, the rifle snapped, and the truck groaned and buckled. They covered their ears but could still hear it. His mother started running toward the house, and they chased after her. Tufts of dune grass scratched their legs, and the girls' flip-flops cracked like distant rifle shots. Yards from the house, Flo turned to him and said, "It means 'shit.' 'Shit's coming.' It's a dirty word."

Cassius stared at her a moment, not knowing quite what she meant. Then he felt anger rising up inside him, hot as a blast furnace. Suddenly he wanted to knock her flat on her bum on the grass.

Flo's eyes widened as if she could read his mind. She hopped off the path and ran for the dirt drive behind the house, and Cassius chased after her, fueled with his anger. She tore around the corner, long hair flapping behind her like a flag.

In the driveway, the Gold's Rambler and the Monroes' Chevy sat baking in the sun. She ducked behind the Chevy, and when he caught up with her, she was crouched beside a rear tire, breathing hard, hands pressed between her thighs. She screamed as he grabbed and pulled her to the pebbled ground. They rolled around in the gritty dirt, while far off, the rifle cracked again and again.

Flo bit his arm and punched his chest, but he finally got her pinned to the driveway. He sat on her legs and held her wrists, twisting them into the dirt, trying to force her to cry. He could see bright bits of sky reflected in her eyes.

"Why won't you cry?" he asked. "Why aren't you crying?"

Her mouth fell open, soft and wet.

"Cry, dammit!"

"No."

"I'll make you!" He shook her wrists, and she stopped fighting, stopped moving completely. She lay there limp and gazing up at him, her eyes two empty pools.

Cassius's ears prickled and his forehead burned. His mouth felt stiff and dry, and his eyes practically disappeared behind their pouchy lids. He waited for Flo to cry, but she wouldn't. She bit her lips hard, not crying.

He finally got off and tried to help her up, but she jerked her arms away. Without glancing back, she hurried for the door. The rifle cracked again, and he stood for a long while in the driveway gazing down the hill at the truck. The crowd had gotten bigger. The whale was lying perfectly still in the flatbed, probably dead. The orange-haired man cocked his gun and pointed it at the whale again.

Cassius dug his hands deep in his shorts' pockets, jiggling the shells there, the loose beach glass. He hung his head and climbed the back stairs, feet punching the weathered wooden treads. "Damn . . . . hell . . . . shit . . . ." he hissed with every step.

He stood in the hallway, catching his breath, and leaned against the boxes of supplies. He could see into the kitchen, where his mother and Mrs. Monroe stood talking. Flo had her head buried in her mother's lap, and she was sobbing. Sobbing! A sudden breeze kicked up, wafting through the screen door and lapping at his backside, while the dirty words kept cracking out of his mouth, little bullets.

The Blue Pontiac

"There's that girl again," Jack said.

"What girl?"

"The one who keeps driving past us." Jack's brother Rick never noticed anything except the TV set when sports were on, or how tall the grass was on everybody's lawn. He read electrical engineering books, wanted to become an electrical engineer. Jack, who was sixteen, wanted to start his own rock band and was teaching himself to play the electric bass. He liked the feeling of power he got, all that sound exploding from his fingertips. Rick helped him rig up an amplifier from an old stereo speaker, but their mother wouldn't let him play for more than an hour at a time since the noise gave her migraines. Rick's only comment was, "Your guitar playing lacks everything but conviction."

"She's been driving all around us," Jack now said, "making a big circle."

Rick squinted at the car idling in front of the World of Flowers and shook his head. "I don't know anyone in a blue Pontiac."

Jack could make out the ember of the girl's cigarette and knew she was watching them, all of them—Jack and Rick, and their friends Travis and Romerez and Pike. They were hanging out at the parking lot of the old shopping plaza that was supposed to be torn down in the fall. This was their corner of the lot until one of the store owners complained; then a cruiser would ease in between the yellow neon entryway signs and glide over to them, cops inside saying, "Okay, fellas, break it up."

So far tonight, though, nobody had bothered to complain. It was getting toward the end of summer, and the cops seemed to have better things to do with their time.

"What's she doing?" Romerez asked, chewing on a toothpick. He had black hair and flashing black eyes and was a senior, like Rick and Pike. Travis, who'd been held back twice, was a sophomore, like Jack.

"Beats me."

"Maybe she will . . . . if you're real nice," Romerez snorted.

Rick pushed his glasses back up his nose and squinted at the girl in the blue Pontiac. Rick had gotten glasses the year after their father died. Lots of strange things happened that year: their mother started working full-time, and they sold the house and moved across town to live in the community housing projects. Rick's eyesight began to weaken, whereas Jack's kept steadily improving. At night, from their sixth floor balcony, he could read highway signs up to as much as half a mile away.

Tonight the air was clear and warm; the stars were out. Jack could smell exhaust fumes from the cars whizzing past on Route 17 and hamburger grease from the Dairy Queen across the way. They were parked in the darkest corner of the lot beside the swamp. That old swamp was full of empty liquor bottles and Dairy Queen wrappers, condoms and bubblegum cards. Sometimes, girls they knew from high school would drive over just to talk to them through the rolled-down window of their daddies' Chevrolets or Subarus, until they got bored, or else scared, and took off. But this was unusual, this strange girl parked about a dozen yards away.

They tried to figure it out while sampling the whiskey-and-orange-juice concoction Travis had mixed in an old Darth Vador thermos.

"Yeoww." Jack made a sour face.

"What's she doing now?" Romerez asked with a deep, perplexed frown.

"Just sittin' there."

"Anybody know her?" Rick asked, and Romerez shoved him; he stumbled a little before righting himself.

"Go find out," Romerez said, and Rick eased his glasses back up the bridge of his nose and returned Romerez's stare. That was the cool thing about Rick; he seemed like such a pushover, but the truth was he'd knocked down a guy almost twice his size at school, and that had given him confidence. Jack envied his older brother; he'd never hit anyone in his life and wasn't looking forward to it, either. If you lived on this side of town, sooner or later you'd have to hit somebody.

Rick worked at the Dairy Queen during the summer months, and Jack did yard work. Rick used his extra cash to buy electrical engineering books and T-shirts printed with inventions by Leonardo da Vinci. The boys shared a bedroom, and Jack would sometimes interrupt Rick's reading to tell him about his plans to start a rock band. He even had a name picked out: Earn Thousands Stuffing Envelopes. Rick would nod his head, only half listening as he flipped through the sports section of the evening paper.

Now Rick said, "I'm going over there and find out what she wants." But the moment he stepped into the cone of yellow light, she gunned her engine and took off, making a wide arc around them. "Hey!" Rick hollered. "Stop!"

But she didn't stop. And Jack could see her face quite clearly through the windshield, and her eyes were wide with panic, as if they'd caught her in the middle of some dirty, private act.

✳

The following night, they were all out at the lot again, and the girl was parked in front of the World of Flowers.

"Hey, I think I know her!" Travis said, gazing at her through a pair of binoculars he'd brought with him from home. "She was in my math class last semester. The new girl, what's her name."

"Oh yeah, whatsername," Romerez sneered. "Good ol' whatsername, the math whiz."

"Kay something."

"Well, if you see Kay, tell her I miss her . . . . Get it? 'If you see Kay?' He doesn't get it."

"Get what?"

"'Get what.' No wonder they held you back."

Another fine night. People as flat as cardboard cutouts emerged from the superette, their skinny arms full of groceries. A young couple swung their little boy between them, and he shrieked with laughter as the red neon letters of the BIG BOWL blinked on and off behind them.

Now Romerez grabbed the binoculars away. "Hey, I can't see a damn thing."

"Gotta adjust the focus, Rome-ear-ass."

"Wait a sec. I see her now. She's looking straight at me. Jeez. She's got blonde hair."

"She was in my math class last year; I'm absolutely positive," Travis said.

"What's she eating?"

"Eatin' this." Pike grabbed his balls, and Romerez hissed through his teeth and knocked him sideways. Then he steadied the binoculars over his eyes again.

"Asshole. She saw. She's gonna leave, I bet."

Travis had a broad wrinkled forehead and large brown eyes. He and Romerez and Pike had already had a couple of girlfriends between them, and Rick had gone out with Sally DeSalisi last year, but Jack had never had a date in his life, unless you counted Cordelia Macaulay, which he didn't. Cordelia was skinny and freckled and told everyone at school she was in love with him.

Late last night, sweaty with lust, Jack had fantasized about the girl in the blue Pontiac. He imagined she'd developed this terrific crush and was following him everywhere—to the video arcade, the gym, while he mowed people's lawns. All day long, he searched for her face among the faces that passed before him.

"She's not eating anything." Travis snatched the binoculars back. "She's smoking a joint."

"No, she isn't."

"Pot shouldn't be illegal, TV should." Pike was on the track team and wore his greasy blonde hair in a ponytail.

Romerez whistled. "Hey, baby, come on over here and let's have a look."

Just then, Rick headed toward the blue Pontiac. He walked deliberately, as if he were moving through water, and Romerez made a bet that she'd speed away soon as Rick's foot hit the rim of the yellow pool of light thrown by the very next streetlamp. But she didn't drive away, even when Rick was engulfed in light. He walked straight up to the Pontiac and stood for a moment on the passenger side while they spoke through the rolled-down window. Then a pale arm reached out of the darkness and opened the door.

"Didja see that?!" Romerez shifted the toothpick from the left- to the righthand side of his mouth. "She opened the door for him!"

Rick didn't even bother to wave as the Pontiac glided across the lot like a silver fish in a murky aquarium.

"Maybe she's a hooker?" Pike said.

"Naw, she was in my *math* class."

"Maybe she's a psycho?" Jack said. "Nyah-ah-ah. Black Widow strikes again."

They smoked cigarettes and pondered the strange girl's identity while Jack made farting sounds with his hands, and somewhere deep in the swamp, a rabbit started shrieking, the worst kind of frightening and lonesome sound.

"Jeeze Louise."

"Somebody turn on some music."

Travis picked up a beer bottle and tossed it into the swamp, and finally there was silence.

"What a drag," Pike grumbled, picking his nose.

Forty minutes passed before the Pontiac returned. They pulled up alongside Travis's van, and Rick leaned over and whispered something into the girl's ear before getting out. Glancing at them shyly, she made a brief, apologetic wave. She had small dark eyes and a small waving hand. Her face was puffy, as if she hadn't been getting enough sleep lately. When she tore out of the lot, the four of them stood gaping.

"Well? So?" Travis rubbed his hands together. "What the hell happened?"

"Yeah, who was she?"

Rick shrugged. "Her name's Katy."

"See? What a memory. Kay . . . . Katy."

"What'd she say?"

Rick rubbed his face. "Nothing much."

"Didja screw her, or what?" Romerez snarled, toothpick jump-ing menacingly.

Rick ignored him, his gaze remaining remote, pinned to vari-ous signs littering the storefront windows. "C'mon, Jack," he said. "Let's go."

That night, in the darkened bedroom they shared, Jack couldn't get Rick to tell him a thing.

"Go to sleep," his older brother said, switching off the light.

*

Saturday was Ironing Day, and every Saturday morning Jack's mother would hang clean clothes in the bathroom and turn the shower on full force; then she'd play musicals on the stereo, *My Fair Lady* or *Hair*, and hum along while she plugged the iron into the overloaded outlet, while hot steam filled the narrow bathroom.

This morning, Jack was sitting on the sofa's broken spine, his back pressed against the faded purple wallpaper. "Ma," he said, waving his hand in front of his face. "I can see that spot again."

"What spot?" She licked her finger, then expertly touched it to the iron.

"That spot that floats around in front of my eyes sometimes."

"Go turn off the shower, Jack."

"When I blink like this, I can see it." He blinked a bunch of times; within his peripheral vision hovered a large red spot, like the residue of a flashbulb.

"Quit blinking then. Could you get the shirts, sweetheart? And get off that couch before you break it."

Jack fetched the shirts for his mother and sat on the arm of the sofa while she ironed first the sleeves, then the collars. She had a system. She also ironed the sheets and pillowcases, spraying every-thing with an atomizer. During the week, she worked at the univer-sity in a biology lab testing cancer cures on rats. Not many of the rats survived, she said.

Three years ago, after Jack's father died, their mother had gone on a rampage and cleaned the house from top to bottom. Jack remembered crawling around under the attic eaves, retrieving boxes of mothball-scented linens and old National Geographic magazines. He and Rick were put to work polishing the silverware and making lists of china and glassware. Then they held a huge yard sale and sold almost everything they owned. Afterwards, they moved into this cramped apartment on the far side of town. Jack wished his mother hadn't sold his childhood toys, things he no longer played with but wouldn't mind still having around—his G.I. Joe dolls, a dusty Erector set, his collection of Tonka trucks.

"Remember when we found that pheasant?" he said now. "And Dad made a splint for its broken wing? We kept it in the shed all winter and fed it oatmeal. Remember?"

"Not really."

"Then we let it go in the spring? Why'd we have to let it go, Ma? It probably got shot. It was tame by then."

His mother's face seemed to shrink toward her pursed lips. Her dark hair was pinned in a careless topknot and her lipstick was smeared at the edges. "Get off the back of the sofa before you break it."

"It's already broken." He hopped off, picked up a baseball and started tossing it from hand to hand. "Remember the time at the drive-in when Rick peed out the back of the station wagon? And everybody was laughing? And Dad got mad . . . . remember?"

"Look," his mother said, hoisting the hot iron and pointing it at him. "Why don't you go clean your room?"

Jack rolled the baseball between his hands.

"Clean your room, like you promised." She blew a few strands of hair from her face and bent over the board, pressing the iron viciously into one of Rick's shirt collars. "Or are you waiting for me to do it? Am I supposed to break my neck all week long working, then come home and pick up after you two?"

Jack went into his room and looked around at the tumbled books and tangled socks. He found his hockey stick and smacked an invisible puck through the mess. He hated making his mother mad, but he hated even more not talking about his father. His mother didn't like to dredge up the past, she said, as if all memories of his father were something they should've sold at the yard sale.

Jack kicked his muddy sneakers underneath his bed, smoothed the blankets, fluffed his pillow, then glanced around, satisfied. He leapt on top of the bed and picked up his bass, a beat-up Fender Jazz Master he bought at a thrift shop for fifty bucks.

Rick was seated at his desk, concentrating on an algebra problem, ridges of his brow multiplying up to the base of his hairline.

"Rick," Jack said, "remember when Dad died?"

"Um." Rick's eyes were narrowed to slits, his fingers pinched white around his pencil.

"What was he wearing?"

Rick shrugged. "Clothes, I guess."

"Ha ha, very funny." Jack rested the bass in his lap. It was fire-engine red and heavy as a tire iron. "He was wearing shorts, wasn't he? It was hot. Early fall."

"Jeans."

"Huh?"

"He was wearing jeans. It wasn't that hot."

"Indian summer, right?"

"And his blue T-shirt."

"And no jacket."

"Nope."

"And his workboots."

"Yup."

"And a five o'clock shadow, 'cause he hadn't shaved."

Rick thought a moment. "Cleanshaven."

"You think he knew?"

"Knew what?"

"He was gonna do it? Or did he just do it without even thinking about it?"

Rick sighed and clapped his book shut. He raised his glasses to the top of his head and rubbed his eyes. Beyond the door, their mother was humming, "I'm Getting Married in the Morning."

"Jesus, Jack. You overanalyze everything to death."

Jack bit his lower lip. He didn't want to overanalyze things to death; he wanted to be cool like his brother.

Whenever Rick yawned, his dark eyes disappeared behind pale folds of flesh and a weird, catlike sound came from his throat. He opened his desk drawer and took out two cigarettes, tossing one over to Jack, who hissed his excitement through his teeth. They put the cigarettes in their mouths and inhaled without lighting up. Rick leaned back in his chair and gazed at the ceiling.

When their mother got to the line about the bells ding-donging, Jack stood on his bed and played air guitar, swinging his arms wildly. Rick laughed so hard, he almost choked.

"I want that room cleaned!" their mother yelled.

"Okay, Ma." He collapsed on the bed and hid the cigarette under his pillow. But just then Rick did something strange—he took out a match and lit his cigarette, then blew smoke rings at the ceiling.

Jack hopped off the bed and opened a window, trying to fan some of the the smoke outside. "What're you doing? Tryin' to get us killed?"

But his brother just sat there smoking the entire cigarette, while their mother turned her record over and started from the beginning again.

Each night in the parking lot, Jack would wait with Rick while he silently rocked back and forth on the balls of his feet. Jack would gaze up and down Route 17 in search of the blue Pontiac. As soon as he'd spotted it, his heart would race and his face would flush and he'd shout, "She's here!" Rick would turn expectantly toward the entranceway, eyes wide with nervous excitement.

Jack tried to see what Katy was wearing that day, whether her hair was pinned or flowing loose over her shoulders. Deep down, he was half in love with her.

Sometimes in the dead of night, when neither of them could

sleep, Jack would press his brother for details, but Rick never revealed much. Katy was from Maryland; she was in Mrs. Schwartz's homeroom; she loved English, hated algebra.

So what? Jack wanted to scream. *What's it like touching her? Kissing her?*

And tonight, standing on the blacktop while the Pontiac pulled away, Jack was afraid to touch himself, as if he might awaken some terrible longing. He wanted to go with them. Why couldn't he go along?

Romerez said, "I'd give my right testicle to find out what they're up to." He looked at Jack and laughed. "Why the hell not?"

They followed the Pontiac across town, taking an unfamiliar back road, a country dead end that led to a stream and field of corn. They parked and crept through the darkness. Jack could make out the black silhouettes of trees. He heard water burbling over rocks. His stomach tensed as if he'd eaten something spicy. They were planning a surprise attack; they'd leap out of the bushes and pound on the car hood with their fists, whooping and hollering like Indians.

The blue Pontiac was parked at the dead end of Crescent Road, tires nudging the cornfield. Jack crept along behind Romerez, whose whistling breath competed with the wind in the trees, the rushing of the stream. As they approached the car, Jack could see them both pretty clearly—Rick was leaning back in his seat, eyes shut, and Katy rested her head on his shoulder. They weren't asleep, but they weren't moving. The car radio was playing some country-western tune, plunky guitar music blending with the chorus of crickets. Rick was stroking Katy's hair, and neither of them spoke.

Jack paused, heart pounding in his chest. He didn't want to invade their private moment together. Turning to Romerez, he signaled him back up the hill with his thumb.

"What?" Romerez hissed as they ran back to the car, feet crunching the crusted dirt. "What's your problem, padre?"

"Shut up," Jack told him, "just shut up and drive."

Back at the lot, Romerez told the others, "She was giving him a blow job. We didn't want to startle them. She might've bitten it off."

Travis clutched his stomach and let out a snort.

"A blow job?" Pike sneered. "That lying sonuvabitch."

"You're full of it, y'know that?" Jack said. Romerez had seen them as clearly as he had, and what it looked like was, she had her ear to Rick's chest and was listening to whatever rhythm was going on inside.

Romerez drew himself up, all six feet. "I'm full of *what?*"

Jack walked away, disgusted.

"Aw, let him go."

"Hey, pussy!" Romerez threw something at Jack's head, but missed, and whatever it was clattered across the asphalt into the pitch black.

✳

All that fall, Jack kept bumping into Rick and Katy in the halls. They were always holding hands, totally absorbed in conversation. Jack could've sworn his brother told Katy more in two minutes than he'd said to him all year.

Rick seemed to have forgotten all about Romerez and Pike, who in turn ignored Jack since he was just a sophomore. At home, Rick acted like a zombie. If he said something, their mother would arch her eyebrows. "He speaks!" she'd say, and that would shut Rick up for good.

Around Halloween, Jack and Travis drove together to the lot. The plaza was deserted, dry leaves blowing across the asphalt. The demolition had already begun. A huge wrecking crane stood like a prehistoric monster over the low, broken storefronts. Jack leaned against an abandoned VW bug and listened to the wind whistling through the stunted trees in the swamp. They were on their second cigarette when they spotted Romerez's puke-green Maverick bouncing over the potholes.

"Hey, assholes," Romerez said cheerfully, stepping out of his car. "Ain't you two supposed to be home studyin', like good little boys?"

Travis kicked an empty Dr. Pepper bottle over to Romerez, who picked it up and tossed it twenty feet into the base of a streetlamp.

Then he looked at the crane and let out a long, sorry sigh that penetrated through to Jack's bones.

"Phew!" he said. "Sure is dead around here."

"Nothing much happening," Travis agreed.

"Nope." Romerez smacked the front fender of his car. "Sure is dead."

✳

Jack heard about the suicide attempt during fifth period. Rick and Katy had skipped class, driven to her parents' house across town, parked the car in the garage, and, with the motor running, fallen asleep in each others' arms. Fortunately, Katy's brother discovered them just in time, and they were both all right.

Jack got called to the principal's, where he sat for five minutes in the outer office on the verge of tears. "Hey, Jack," somebody said, "your brother tried to shoot himself? 's that true?"

Then the principal explained what really happened—that his brother was okay, that his mother wanted him home immediately.

Jack and his mother visited Rick every day in the psychiatric wing of the hospital. Rick looked all twisted up inside, his face swollen with anguish. He kept begging their mother to let him see Katy.

"Her parents don't think it's such a good idea, and frankly I agree with them," she said. "How could you, Rick? How could you hurt me like this?"

In the psychiatric wing, all the clocks told a different time. "They won't shut up," Rick complained about the doctors who examined him, his eyes red-rimmed and wild. "They keep asking me what it's like to die. What do they want to know that for? One of them told me Thomas Edison never graduated from grade school. Who the hell cares?"

On their visits, Jack's mother would bring shopping bags full of lasagne and whole wheat rolls, apples and fresh-baked muffins. Rick hardly touched a thing, his fingers nervously leafing through the pages of a book or else running up and down the edges of his slide rule.

The few times they were alone together, Jack would turn to Rick and say, "C'mon, you can trust me. What'd you do it for?"

"I dunno."

"But you didn't mean to kill yourself, right?"

"Yeah, right."

"You're okay and everything, right?"

"Did you bring me my math assignment?"

"Sure," Jack said. "But you're okay?"

"Yeah."

"You're okay and everything, right?"

"Yeah, right."

After Rick was released, things fell pretty much into place the way they'd always been, except that Rick and Katy were forbidden to see each other. "Not ever?" Rick cried.

The following Friday night, their mother left for her Bingo game, reminding them to stay out of trouble. "I mean it, buster," she told Rick. "No funny stuff." She planted wet kisses on their foreheads and left.

"Now what you're going to do is," Rick said as soon as she was gone, "call that creepy friend of yours, Cornelia . . . ."

"Cordelia? She's not my friend."

"And set up a meeting between me and Katy tonight."

"Katy? But Mom just said . . . ."

"Who cares what Mom says? What does Mom know?"

Cordelia was happy to do Jack a favor, and he had the funny feeling she'd hold it over his head, but he didn't let that stop him. His brother needed him. Cordelia called back to tell him the meeting was all set. Then Rick got Travis to drive them to Katy's house across town near the dairy farms, where the houses were big and white and had the kind of vast green lawns that boys like Jack got hired to mow in the summertime.

It was frosty out. Jack's throat grew hoarse from the cigarettes they were smoking. Travis parked his Camaro about three blocks from Katy's house, and they just sat there, waiting.

"She'd better come," Rick said glumly.

"She'll be here. Cordelia said she'd be here." Jack cracked his window an inch.

"She'd better."

After a while, they spotted a figure heading toward them—a girl, a blonde. It was Katy, walking a small, sausagelike dog.

Rick hopped out of the car, and they kissed while the dog barked and snapped at his heels. They laughed and started to talk, and soon they were arguing. Jack rolled down his window to catch a few words. "My father . . . . he won't . . . . let's try . . . . we can't . . . ."

Katy kept shaking her head, yanking on the dog's leash, while Rick fumed and paced and blew smoke out his nose. Then Jack heard him say, "Did you tell them we'd never do it again?"

"Yes!" Katy's voice was shrill.

"Well, they can't keep us apart. Nobody can!"

"My father would kill me. He'd have a heart attack."

"Make up your mind," Rick said, "who would it kill? Him or you?"

Katy's hands flew up as if she'd been shot, and the dog lurched furiously at Rick. "Stop it, Snoots!" she said.

"*Snoots?*" Travis laughed.

"Shh." Jack drew his head inside as his brother came charging back to the car. Katy was already halfway down the block.

"Go!" Rick said, slamming the door.

"What happened?"

"Shut up and drive."

They stopped at a liquor store, where they convinced some guy to buy them a bottle, then headed out of town and drove around the countryside for a while, until Rick hollered, "Stop!"

They were out in the middle of nowhere, dairy farms and stubbled cornfields. They sat in the car, shivering and passing the bottle around. Jack didn't understand his brother anymore. Their breath made condensation on the windows, and Jack rubbed a hole in the condensation and peered out at the stars. The sky was black and incredibly clear. "I feel tiny," he said, "like a bird that can't fly."

Rick breathed smoke in Jack's face. "She hates my guts," he said. "And guess whose idea the whole thing was?"

"C'mon, what're you talking about?"

Rick got out of the car.

"Where you goin'?"

Jack and Travis followed Rick outside, and the three of them staggered around in the dark, laughing and puffing out ghosts with their breath.

"Remember how dad used to swear?" Rick said. "And Mom couldn't stand it? The worst she ever says is *cripes.*"

"Oh heck!" Jack laughed. "Oh poop!"

"Remember we used to name cars?" Rick said. "Green Gator. Rusty Muscle."

"Smoking Gun."

For a second, Jack almost forgot how to breathe.

"Help!" Travis fell over something, and they rushed to his side.

At the edge of the cornfield lay a pumpkin patch, thick curls of dried grass and black vines netting the pumpkins, their sides soft and rotting. Jack picked one up and threw it into the field where it landed with a thud, spilling a bellyful of seeds.

"Hey," Rick said. "I got an idea."

They loaded up the car with pumpkins, then drove back to Katy's house. The blue Pontiac was parked in the driveway. Rick got out and crouched behind the Camaro, while Jack handed him pumpkins through the window. One by one, Rick chucked the pumpkins at the Pontiac. They hit the blue metal with a thud, pulp and seeds covering the doors and long hood. Unripe pumpkins bounced off the roof and rolled across the driveway like guillotined heads.

Rick hurled an enormous pumpkin at the house. It squashed on the cement steps, and the porch light blinked on.

Jack crouched down inside the Camaro, while Travis gunned the engine. "C'mon, get in!"

Rick stood for a moment in the middle of the road, squinting at the front door, now opening. Katy's father stood on the threshold—a big barrel-chested man in a canary-yellow turtleneck. He looked out at the dark night and assessed the damage.

"Rick!" Travis called.

Rick held Katy's father's eye for a long moment. "You gonna shoot me?" he asked. When her father didn't respond, Rick placed his hands over his heart. "Agghhh! I'll never walk again!"

They peeled out of the driveway, laughing. "Did you see the look on his face?" Rick said in a choked, hysterical voice. "Didja see?" The car reeked of pumpkins now.

Jack shut his eyes, suddenly exhausted. Everything faded—their voices, the thrumming of the engine, the passing scenery. He couldn't help but feel sorry for Katy's father, the way he'd stood with one hand on the doorknob, as if he were a little bit afraid of them. And his brother kept laughing and swearing, sounding more like Romerez than himself.

When they got home, their mother was waiting up, leaning against the kitchen stove, an eerie light cast across her face.

"You're drunk," she hissed.

"Mom, we . . . ."

"You're late, and you're drunk, and guess who just called?" She grabbed Rick's jacket sleeve but he jerked away. "I trusted you! I told you to take care of your little brother, and now look what you've done. He's as drunk as a skunk!"

Jack giggled.

"Go to your room," she said, jabbing Jack's arm.

"Sorry, Ma."

"Go!"

Jack felt along the wall for the light switch. Kicking off his shoes, he landed facedown in bed, his mother's voice still buzzing around inside his head. The room glowed faintly blue.

He didn't know how much time had passed before his brother was with him in the room. "So you can't see Katy anymore?" Jack asked.

"I don't care."

"What?"

Rick stood swaying for a moment. "I don't love her anymore." And he collapsed on his unmade bed.

※

Whenever Jack spotted Katy in the halls after that, she pretended not to recognize him. His heart would race during assemblies or pep rallies as he searched for her face—the small dark eyes, the long blonde curl of her hair. He didn't have the guts to talk to her, though. What would he say?

That summer, Rick got admitted into college early, and Jack took his old job at the Dairy Queen. Romerez graduated from high school and became assistant manager of the Shoe Tree in the new mall. It was funny, Romerez working in the mall like a regular person instead of being chased away for loitering.

One morning at the Shoe Tree, Jack and Romerez were arguing about the size of Jack's feet, when all of a sudden he thought he saw Katy walking by. Only she must have gained about thirty pounds, because he hardly recognized her.

Romerez bet it wasn't Katy, so Jack followed her down the brightly lit corridor, staying just out of sight. Her big round hips swayed beneath the thin blue dress, and she seemed to be moving with a purpose. She didn't glance into any of the store windows, just kept walking through the crowd of people streaming all around her.

She paused in front of a bakeshop window, and Jack finally had a chance to study her profile—same small dark eyes, same pretty round face, long blonde hair curving across her cheek—and he knew for sure it was Katy. Only she looked about five years older. Her breasts stuck way out beneath the fabric of her blue dress, and she had a double chin.

She caught him watching, and her face flushed. He could tell she didn't want to be recognized, especially not by Rick's younger brother. She gave him a pained, embarrassed look, then strode away, big hips bouncing.

Romerez was waiting for Jack by the display sign, a tree sprouting sneakers. "So . . .?"

"It wasn't her," Jack said, brushing past.

"You sure? I could've sworn . . . ."

Jack wished he'd had the guts to say something. He would've told Katy that to him, she'd always be the girl in the blue Pontiac, and that his brother probably loved her in some secret part of himself, and that whatever they'd done wasn't anybody's fault. And that the mall, the goddamn mall, would always be a run-down, crumbling wreck.

"Hey, where you goin'?" When Jack didn't answer, Romerez shouted, "You owe me ten bucks, amigo!"

Jack took the fire stairs down. Reaching the second-floor landing, it suddenly hit him: he was standing on the exact spot that used to be the old pet shop. The owner was this old Armenian guy with a thick black mustache who was always dribbling mayonnaise on his chin from the tuna fish sandwiches he ate. He used to let them play with the kittens and puppies, or else they'd watch him feed the python he kept in a glass case in the window. And Jack remembered how the place used to smell—old turtle water and birdseed mixed with sawdust. And he had a vivid image of the pet shop, of all the animals that had come and gone, and he thought about the customers from the old shopping plaza walking around in this shiny new mall, how their pasts were like shadows on the linoleum floor. And something lit up inside of him; it was as if everybody's fears and dreams and longings exploded right inside his chest.

But then, just as quickly, the feeling was gone.

Jack gripped the banister and went flying the rest of the way down. He stumbled out of the cardboard-smelling darkness into the bright sunshine, running past station wagons and flatbed trucks and empty grocery carts, kids and blue-haired old ladies, toward the farthest corner of the lot, where he kicked an empty condensed milk can high into the air and watched as it landed in the middle of the swamp.

Puddle Tongue

"I don't want to talk about it," Willa insisted, signing *no, no, no* in Dori's face, her hand forming the head of a duck, her fingers making its bill go quack, quack, quack.

"But I thought you wanted to go to college?" Dori was trying to sign and drive at the same time, a dangerous activity. Her deaf cousin had just arrived with all her worldly goods packed in a box and two suitcases. She'd traveled seven hours by bus, she was sunburned and tired, and already they were having an argument.

"To Gaulladet? Grandma Rose said . . . ." Dori faced Willa so she could read her lips. There'd once been a time when Willa had been able to pick out the melodies of her favorite songs, but she'd lost her hearing completely by age twelve.

"No," Willa said emphatically. "I'm not going to school. I'll get a job, become part of the *real world*." She circled her hands, one over the other, extending them far before her, as if the world were unimaginably vast.

They stopped at an intersection, and Dori signed with her hands. "But Gaulladet will help you learn to live in the real world better."

"Your signing's gotten sloppy," was all Willa said. She had a syrupy lisp, the words coming out soft and damp-sounding, muted as notes blown from an old clarinet whose pads had never been changed. She twisted around to get a better look at the baby.

Dori hadn't seen Willa in three years. Two round white circles where her sunglasses had been made her look like a reverse raccoon. Her long, dark hair was pulled into a sloppy ponytail, held in place by glow-in-the-dark barrettes, and she wore a pair of faded

overalls and earrings shaped like tiny pineapples. Although Dori
was six years older, they'd grown up close as sisters just three blocks
apart in a small Rhode Island town. Neither of them had any brothers or sisters, so they turned to one another for companionship. Willa
had been precocious as a child, talking excitedly about boys and art
and horseback riding. She never understood it when Dori bolted
from the bed to answer the telephone, interrupting their intimate
conversations. Dori the Phone Slave, she called her.

"Ssssweetie pi-iee," Willa cooed, waving at the sleeping baby.
"Hello there . . . ."

"Shhh!" Dori poked her ribs. "It took me half an hour to put her
down. She'll be awake soon enough." Two-year-old Emily was an-
gelic in sleep, her blonde hair forming peaks as soft as meringue all
over her head.

"Oops. Sorry." Willa propped her arm out the window.

Dori had almost forgotten the silence of the deaf; she was at
liberty to whisper, or simply to mouth her words—Willa was an
expert lip-reader.

"Okay," she said, "no more talk about school, long as you promise we'll discuss it at the end of the summer."

"What for?"

"To decide about your future."

"Who says I need a future?"

There were dime-sized holes in Willa's overalls where her sunburned skin showed through a fringe of white threads. She wore a
pair of purple high-tops similar to the ones she'd shown up in at
Dori's wedding, three years earlier. High-tops and a satin brides-
maid's gown, creating a last-minute flurry of activity, a mad dash
for an extra pair of pumps—any color—that would fit her size-seven
feet. Dori's mother had threatened to kick Willa out of the proces-
sion until, in despair, she had squeezed into a borrowed pair of heels
and limped down the aisle behind them.

"Just promise," Dori said now.

Willa faced the breeze. Her T-shirt sleeves were rolled up, and
on her inner arm she'd drawn a lightning-bolt tattoo, blue ink spreading outward in feathery threads.

"Okay, cuzzzz," she said, drawing out the last word until it sounded like an admonishment.

✳

Dori's husband Tom had spent the last few weeks learning phrases from a sign language book he'd picked up in town. He could sign "I'm hungry," "thank you," "excuse me," and "you're pretty." But the first thing he told her was, "We want you to feel welcome," his hands moving gracefully through the air.

"Let's get drunk," Willa suggested.

Dori laughed. "Let's try some of that pot Grandma Rose got so upset about." Last month, Grandma Rose had called to ask them if they'd take Willa in for the summer, before she went away to school. "She's too much teenager for me to handle," she'd explained. During her last semester at high school, Willa had been caught shoplifting at K-Mart and smoking pot with friends in Special Needs.

"Not funny, Dori," Tom said, frowning.

"What a poop," Dori signed. "'Not funny,' he says, as if we've never smoked a joint in our lives."

"What're you telling her?"

"Don't worry, Tom," Willa said, a sly smile plying her lips. "I've gone straight. I've learned my lesson."

"Tom forgets how wild he and I used to be," Dori said, "before we had the baby."

"Oh, no, I remember." Grinning, he took her hand.

"We used to go skinny-dipping at Wakami Lake."

Willa's eyes lit up. "Where's that?"

"Up the road a bit."

"Can we go swimming tomorrow?"

"Sure." Dori helped her carry the stereo speakers out onto the porch, where they pointed them at the woods. They turned up the bass, frightening the night creatures long used to their considerate silence. Willa kicked off her shoes and, feeling the pulsating beat of the drums through the soles of her feet, began to dance. Eyes shut, she slowly gyrated, making small, sinewy movements.

"How'd you learn to dance?" Tom asked, and she pantomimed what she imagined to be music—fluttering her hands through the air, kicking her legs to the beat—then patted her chest.

"Music in my heart," she lisped.

"Remember when Aunt Lo wanted the two of us to study chess?" Dori signed. "Instant rebellion."

"I don't want to talk about the past."

Dori's arms collapsed by her sides. Not talk about the past? How could they not talk about the past? Dori had protected her cousin against the ugly threats of neighborhood bullies, while Willa had taught Dori how to sign and take risks. She'd been the bravest kid Dori had ever known, always climbing to the highest branch of a tree. Dori showed Willa how to insert her first tampon, and once, in an intimate act of friendship, they even touched tongues.

"Willa, tell Tom about the time . . . ."

"No," she said, her posture defiant. "No going back." She took a seat beside the baby and played with her blue-and-yellow plastic keys. "No more 'remember whens . . . .'"

✳

Five hours later, Dori still couldn't sleep. She listened to her husband's ragged breathing, watched his milky chest as it rose and fell. He was fair-skinned, with silky blonde eyelashes and reddish hair—not strawberry blonde or carrot-topped, but the red of an Irish setter's coat.

After three years of marriage, she still hadn't gotten used to his snoring. They'd met at an art gallery on Newbury Street. She was working as a secretary for a Boston advertising firm, and he was a carpenter at a local college. He'd stared at her over his glass of champagne, and she remembered thinking how lovely his eyes were, clear as settled lake water. They talked for hours, then he took her back to his Allston apartment, where they made love on a foam rubber mattress. His room smelled of varnish and cedar oil, and he touched her in ways she imagined he'd sand an important bit of woodwork.

Now her gaze roamed aimlessly across the ceiling, where there were no water spots, no chips of paint, nothing to latch onto. The full moon made midnight seem like the dusty moments before dawn. She listened to owls hooting back and forth, the repetitive cry of peepers down by the swamp. Willa was out back in the camper, parked just a dozen yards from the house. Painted lime-green, it squatted on cement blocks, awaiting renovation. Tom had picked it up dirt cheap from a retired couple who'd traveled across America, only to settle here, in Porterville.

Before picking Willa up at the bus depot, Dori had vacuumed the camper's insides, scrubbed the small sink and toilet, made the bed with flannel sheets and propped three pillows against the moss-green wall. Then she stood there thinking about Willa's old bedroom with its pictures of horses taped to the walls, her stuffed animal collection, the bookshelves and comfortable quilts, and how none of it existed any longer.

Now the baby was stirring. Dori slipped out of bed and drew on her terrycloth robe, the one with the lozenges stuck in the pockets. The floor felt cool for June. She made her way through the moonlit hall into the nursery, where Emily slept soundly, wrapped in baby dreams and her two-year-old smell. Dori leaned over the crib and patted her backside while she breathed noisily onto the sheeted mattress. She'd have Tom's allergies, Dori predicted, his humming snore.

She stood beside the open bedroom window a moment to gaze up at the moon, ripe and white and ready to drop. It lit the whole back yard and made the lime-green camper shimmer. Down below, past the coiled hose, the garden fence and rectangles of lawn chairs, she caught a furtive movement by the stone wall. Suddenly, something shot out of the bushes, then pirouetted past the camper's front fender. Dori's pulse points throbbed. She recognized her cousin, Willa, spinning around the lawn like a water sprite, like a whirling dervish.

Emily whimpered in her sleep, then startled awake. Her cries were like puncture wounds—sharp and clean and slow to bleed. Dori cradled her daughter in her arms, feeling her small body tremble with indignation, or else discomfort. She remembered how, when they were young, Willa was the only one brave enough to leap off the rocky overhang at Cedar Lake. Her wildness always amazed Dori; it seemed as if the regular rules didn't apply to her.

By the time Dori had soothed Emily back to sleep, Willa was nowhere in sight.

✳

Willa slouched over her plate at the kitchen table, playing with her lunch. Her hair was pulled into a ponytail so tight, her eyes seemed slanted. She wore a halter top and the kind of vibrant, baggy shorts an old man might retire in. "Why didn't you come to the funeral?" she asked.

"Like I explained in my letter, we had to stay with the baby."

"But the funeral . . . ." Willa's forehead knotted with an old hurt.

Dori, suddenly realizing she'd been avoiding this subject, took a deep breath, her neck growing hot. "Emily's life was hanging by a thread," she signed, placing her pinkie fingers together. "She could've died."

"But she didn't."

Crossing her arms, Dori tried to stifle her rising anger. She didn't want to remember that time. The baby had been placed in an incubator, where she'd breathed with the aid of a respirator. Her sheets and blankets were hospital white, and Dori remembered thinking what a tiny thing she was within all that whiteness.

News of the fire reached them at the hospital. Dori broke down, and the doctor had to give her a sedative. Tom called Grandma Rose, sent flowers, but they stayed with their child as she struggled to survive.

The fire started in the basement of Dori's aunt and uncle's house in the middle of the night. Within half an hour, flames had reached the first floor and were creeping up the stairwell. When the second floor was engulfed in smoke, Willa flung herself out her bedroom window and broke her right leg in two places—a lucky fall, the doctors said. She could've snapped her neck. Aunt Lo and Uncle Jeff both died in their sleep before the flames even reached their bedroom.

"Brrr-rrrnnnnggg!" Willa now shrieked, picking up Emily's pink play phone. "See? I remember. Dori, the Phone Slave." She held the toy phone to her ear, and Dori couldn't help smiling. Willa spoke mutely into the mouthpiece, making the most exasperated faces, and Emily laughed gleefully and tossed her arms. "For you," Willa said, handing it over.

"We couldn't leave the baby's side. You understand, don't you?" Dori felt a surge of resentment clogging her throat and shifted around on the creaky kitchen chair. "You know I would've come if it were at all possible."

"Arrghh," Willa said, wrapping the pink phone cord around her neck, pretending to choke herself.

Dori got up and tossed her coffee down the drain. "I've got to rake the garden," she said.

Willa hadn't heard, of course. Dori tapped her on the shoulder. "Want to help? Outside?"

The air smelled faintly salty. Blue treetops tumbled toward them along the horizon like ocean waves. Dori handed Willa a bottle of sunscreen, but she brushed it aside.

"I'm going to find a job," she said. "I don't want you and Tom giving me everything." She made the sign for "take, take, take," drawing both hands toward her chest. "I'm on my own now. A big girl."

Dori dragged the rake thoughtfully over the crusted soil, metal teeth catching on embedded twigs. She gave it a tug, and a pink stone the size of a walnut loosened from the dirt and rolled toward Emily's foot. Emily tossed it toward the lime-green camper.

"Fine," Dori told her, "get a job. That way, in the fall, you'll have a little spending money for college."

"I told you not to mention that!" Willa's face turned red, and she bolted from the garden, accidentally knocking over the plank that served as a gate for the chicken wire fence.

"Willa!"

As she disappeared into her camper, Dori had to remind herself that her cousin didn't hold a monopoly on pain and suffering. Emily plucked an earthworm from the overturned soil and brought it to her mouth.

"No, sweetie. Don't." Dori took the worm and tossed it so far away she couldn't see where it landed.

✳

The Hurryback Cafe was shoebox-shaped and painted a cheery yellow. The owner, Sally, was an old friend of Dori's. As they entered the diner, a counterful of men as big as bears glanced up, then slouched back over their food, arms curled protectively around their plates.

"How's the little one?" Sally asked, hefting a scalding basket of water glasses onto the stainless steel counter. She tickled Emily's chin. "Hey there, cutie."

"Sally, I'd like you to meet my cousin, Willa."

"Howdy, Willa!"

"No need to shout. She can read lips."

Gray-haired and beefy-armed, Sally gave a generous smile. "How d'you like Maine so far?"

Willa shrugged. "Okay, I guess."

"You a hard worker?"

Willa nodded.

"How soon can you start?"

"Any time."

"Tomorrow at eight soon enough?"

Willa nodded again, and they shook hands.

"Maybe Dori can help you find a uniform out back?"

"Simple enough, huh?" Dori signed as they rummaged through the box of pink uniforms.

That night, they celebrated with a bottle of Blue Nun. Tom, wielding an invisible straw hat and cane, tapdanced over the lawn. "Overture! Curtain! Lights!" Willa, straddling the picnic bench, laughed shrilly each time he kicked one of his stork-thin legs. He pried Dori from the yellow lawn chair and twirled her around, while Emily gaped at them from her bouncy seat.

Willa rummaged through the radio stations until she found a heavy metal tune that hit the air with a thud, drums and bass thundering across the deck like split boulders, the lead singer's voice a screeching needlescrape.

"Good Lord." Dori clasped her hands over her ears while Tom tried to keep pace with Willa's frantic gyrations. The sudden jolt of noise startled the baby, whose face lost its confidence like a deflating balloon. And soon, above the chugging guitars came Emily's sea gull cries.

✳

Starlight filled the windows, reminding Dori of long-ago summer nights when the dogs would bark across Cedar Lake, and she and Willa would get up at the crack of dawn to go swimming. Dori always back-stroked out to the middle, while Willa took a different route, leaping from the rocky drop at the northernmost tip. Her daring always frightened Dori, but she never dreamed of stopping her.

Now Dori touched Tom's shoulder, gently prying him from sleep. "We talked about the funeral today. I think she's still mad at us for not going."

Something in the house creaked. Tom burrowed further into his pillow, letting out a sigh she could feel against her shoulder. When he wasn't doing landscaping and gardening at the university, he was down in the basement making furniture, his hands permanently stained the color of maple.

"We did our best, under the circumstances."

"I'm not so sure."

He rubbed his face sleepily. "Don't be ridiculous. Emily needed us."

"But even when the worst was over?"

Tom let out an exhausted yawn.

"I was terrified, Tom. For months afterward—did you know?— I used to count things. How many bottles left in the refrigerator, how many times Emily cried during the night. 'Even' was good. 'Odd' was bad. I always let the phone ring twice before picking it up. Or else four times. If it stopped on three, I'd panic."

He wrapped her in his arms, kissed her forehead. He held her tightly for a moment before letting his grip slip. "Try and get some sleep," he murmured, the bed bouncing with his shifting weight. Her emotions were all stirred up with no place to go. She lay very still, tracing the dark slope of his shoulder. "Tom?"

But he was already snoring. And soon, she felt herself beginning to breathe in time to his jagged rhythm.

✳

On Friday morning, Dori got a call from Sally. "We need to talk," she hissed. "But first, is Willa there with you? Just answer, yes or no."

"She's out back with Emily." Dori glanced through the kitchen window just to make sure, then cupped her hand over the mouthpiece. "Sally, what is it? What's wrong?"

"She's been stealing things . . . ."

Dori caught her breath, not certain she'd heard right. "What?"

"From the diner. I've seen her myself. She swiped an ashtray right off the table, stuck it in her apron pocket. Look, there's money missing. I don't care about ashtrays, but the money . . . ."

"Wait a minute, Sally, slow down." Willa was squatting beside Emily in the back yard, showing her how the fire engine's hook and ladder worked. "Are you absolutely certain?"

"Sure as I can be. One of my girls spotted her, too."

"Have you confronted her yet?"

"No. I thought I'd leave that up to you."

"Thanks, Sally. I'll get back to you."

Willa was making cooing sounds, stroking Emily's cheek. Dori's fingers shook as she rinsed her hands in the sink. She stepped outside and tapped Willa on the shoulder. "Would you mind going into town for some milk?"

"Sure." She leapt to her feet, wiped her hands on the back of her overalls, and bounded toward the garage where they kept their bikes. She left behind two cigarette butts and a faint whiff of smoke.

Once she was gone, Dori leaned against the swingset and tried to still her racing heart. She took measured steps, hesitating in the camper doorway. Her eyes slowly adjusting to its shadowy interior.

The bed was neatly made. Willa's clothes hung from a line strung across the walls of the tiny kitchen. It was so sad, the whole thing—the way she'd piled her books against the far wall, the way she let the sun burn her, the holes in her clothes, the ease with which Dori had been able to deceive her.

Now Dori took a deep breath and fumbled through the cabinets, the narrow closet packed with shoes, Willa's suitcases and the cardboard box she'd brought with her from home. The suitcases were empty. The box was full of personal belongings—books and magazines and a bag of makeup, a singed stuffed zebra, two orange eyes staring out from its ancient, matted fur.

Kneeling beside the bed, she lifted the hem of the quilt. A gray box was pushed up against the far wall. With a sinking feeling, she slid it toward her and unfolded the flaps. The box was full of supplies from the diner—empty sugar containers, those ugly metal ashtrays, salt-and-pepper shakers shaped like tiny boots. There was a beat-up wooden spatula, dozens of packets of Sweet 'n Low and three empty ketchup bottles. Outside, a warm breeze shouldered the camper walls, making the metal spouts on the sugar containers rattle and tick.

"What am I doing?" Dori gasped, hairs on her arms goosepimpling. She slid the box back under the bed, positioning it the same way she'd found it. Then she smoothed the sides of the quilt, taking exquisite care so that no one would ever guess she'd been there.

✳

"Why don't you stay out of the sun? At least use a sunscreen."

Willa's face and arms were raw-looking after her shower. Slick strands of hair clung to her neck. She had Uncle Jeff's concave profile, all cheekbones and chin.

"You'll get sun poisoning."

"I'm all right." She slouched forward, elbows planted on the table. Dori didn't know how to bring up Sally's accusations. She didn't even know how to broach the subject. Her stomach was clenched as an angry fist. Willa kept lighting matches, letting them burn down as far as they could go and then dropping them in an empty butter dish. An unlit cigarette dangled between her lips.

"Remember when I tried to sneak cigarettes at Aunt Lo's? I'd hide in the bathroom, but you'd bang on the door until I flushed them down the toilet. Smoking's bad for your health, you said."

"I was right." The next match singed her fingers.

"Please talk to me. Tell me about that night."

"What night?"

"You know."

"There's nothing to tell." Willa tossed the empty matchbook on the table, and Dori felt her anger like a slap.

"Look," Dori said. "My whole life was crumbling before my eyes. First the baby, then Aunt Lo and Uncle Jeff . . . . I just thanked God you were all right."

Willa picked up the matchbook and stirred it around in the butter dish, where bits of butter and spent matches turned into an ashen soup. "In the emergency room," she signed carefully, "I watched them wheel my mother in. Her face was burnt; it was awful. She was burnt to a crisp. I've heard that expression all my life, but I never knew what it really meant. She opened her eyes and looked at me. Dr. Muncie says it's impossible, that I must've dreamt it, because she was dead even before they brought her in. But I swear, she looked at me and smiled. Then I blacked out.

"When I woke up, my leg was in a cast, and I was in the hospital room, and the lights were very bright. Grandma Rose sat beside me. She asked, did I want anything? And the only thing I could think of was milk. I asked for a glass of milk, which is weird, because I've always hated milk. You know that, don't you?"

"Yes." She nodded her fist.

"I've always hated milk."

A blue jay cawed outside. Willa's face sagged at the corners, as if something inside of her, some vital structure, had collapsed. She grabbed her cigarettes and ran from the kitchen. Dori anticipated the slamming of the camper door, and when it came, her spine jerked.

She got up to dump the spent matches along with the remainder of Willa's tuna sandwich down the garbage disposal. Willa's being sent to stay with them, she suddenly realized, was Grandma Rose's idea of punishment. Because of the pot, because of the shoplifting, because of her uncontainable grief. Grandma Rose's house was spotless, filled with the kind of knickknacks Dori and Willa always joked about—little leprechauns leaning against ceramic toadstools, a cow whose tail formed the handle of a creamer. Dori couldn't imagine constantly having to inhale the scent of Pinesol and lemon-fresh Pledge.

Leaning against the sink, she felt the vibrations of the disposal through her hip. Did she even have the right, she wondered, to ask what Willa had hidden in the box beneath her bed?

✳

After dinner, the four of them drove to the dump and parked on the outskirts near a rotting armchair. This was Tom's idea of entertainment, looking for bears.

"When it's dark," he explained, pronouncing his words very carefully, "if we're lucky, the bears will come and start foraging for food. Then, at just the right moment, I'll switch on the headlights."

Tom didn't know about Willa's thievery; they hadn't had a chance to discuss it, but Dori believed he could sense her tension. He opened a bottle of burgundy, while she fished around in her bag for paper cups. She wanted to get roaring drunk. She wanted to forget she had any responsibilities at all. Emily rested in her lap, pacifier stuck in her mouth like a TV knob. The sky had lost its pink, its baby blue, and was now cobalt, and flat as a painted canvas. They could see stars. Black trees swayed in the wind, making airplanes appear to hover and zigzag across the horizon.

"Look," Tom said, "a UFO. D'you believe in UFO's, Willa?"

"That's just an airplane." Dori nudged him with her knuckles, then signed the question back.

"All my life," Willa admitted, "I wanted to be swooped up into a UFO."

"Me, too." He tilted back his head to drink.

"UFO's don't exist," Dori said, wanting to pop their balloon. "Even Carl Sagan says so."

"He didn't say they don't exist, Dori. He just said we're so fucking far out of the way, nobody wants to bother. We're just this tiny, insignificant speck on the tail of some minor galaxy." He pinched his fingers together to demonstrate.

"Well, I like insignificant places. Like Porterville."

Willa leaned forward. "Can I hold the baby?" Her eyes were in shadow, a slant of moonlight highlighting the patches of peeling skin over her nose and chin.

"She's almost asleep." Dori felt her fingers tighten around the blanket.

"I'll be careful."

Dori shifted Emily from arm to arm before reluctantly handing her back, and Emily began to protest in that squeaky-toy way of hers.

"Aw, don't be glum, chum," Willa cooed, and Dori's throat constricted. When they were young, a neighborhood brat once taunted Willa with the nickname "Puddle Tongue," and she burst into tears. Dori had never heard her cry so long or so hard before. She chased the bully back inside his house, but Willa kept on crying all afternoon. Finally, Aunt Lo took her head in her lap and smoothed the hair from her face, whispering, "Don't be glum, chum." Over and over.

Cradling the baby in her arms, Willa whispered things Dori couldn't understand. Her tongue flapped noisily against the roof of her mouth, dead air squeezing out between her teeth. She reminded Dori of a windup toy knocked on its side, all clacking, laboring mechanics.

"There's one!" Tom cried, switching on the brights.

"Where?"

"Over there!"

All she could see were a pair of wide, red eyes blinking in the headlights' glare.

Dori turned to Willa and signed, "See that? Just like your stuffed zebra. Do his eyes still glow in the dark?"

Willa sat up, rigid. Dori suddenly realized her mistake, but before she had a chance to explain, Willa reached for the door handle and, in one swift move, bolted from the car with the baby in her arms.

"Willa!"

Dori hurled herself out into the night, feet landing hard against the uneven ground. Emily's sobs wobbled to the beat of Willa's fading footsteps. Moonlight painted the piles of trash silver, soap-yellow.

"Willa!" Dori shrieked.

Willa stopped a few yards short of the exit where the streetlights were brightest. Emily's cries shrank to whimpering gasps. The dump smelled of burnt things, rotten things. Low fires glowed like bears' eyes, blinking open and shut. They could've been surrounded right now, dozens of bears prowling behind the mounds of trash and smoky, discarded furniture.

"Willa, give me the baby!" Dori gasped, struggling to compose herself. "Hand me my baby!" She cradled an invisible infant in her arms.

Far away, a car door slammed. "Dori?" Tom called.

Emily's head was slumped against Willa's shoulder.

"Hand me the baby, Willa."

"That's all you care about!"

"Just give me the baby, and we'll discuss it."

"Discuss what? What could we possibly talk about? You don't even know who I am anymore!"

Dori took a careful step forward, fingers straining ahead. "I know who you are. You're my cousin. My little sister."

Willa's face contorted with pain.

"I'm sorry," Dori signed, frantic. "I'm sorry, Willa, but it's not my fault they died. It's not my fault that the baby was premature. What on earth can I say to make things right between us?" Dori made the sign for suffer, twisting her fist in front of her mouth. "Both of us," she signed, "have suffered."

Willa jostled Emily in her arms as her hands flew through the air. "You never even bothered to visit me after my parents died. What do you care? Two years, I waited. Two whole years, Dori!"

Dori's stomach contracted as if she'd been punched. "Willa, please . . . ." She took a step forward. "The baby . . . ."

"Don't you trust me? What d'you think I'm going to do? Hurt her?"

Just then, Tom sprang from the smoky darkness and snatched Emily away. He let out a yelp of triumph as Willa propelled herself into the night, a wild thing.

Tom cradled the baby in his arms while Dori counted her toes, examined her nose, her eyes, her knees. Dori's hands were trembling. Emily squirmed, wanting to be let down, wide awake now and no longer afraid.

"Willa! Willa!" Tom hollered.

"She can't hear you."

"What the hell just happened?"

Willa's receding footsteps hit the dirt with a repetitive thud. Their daughter, they soon discovered, was fine. Perfectly fine.

✳

Dori waited upstairs in the baby's room while Tom went searching for Willa. She watched the road through a veil of trees; whenever a car drove past, slender saplings leapt out of the darkness, their shadows fanning wider and wider in the receding headlights' glare. Once the car had passed, the woods blinked off. A network of crickets chirped their perpetual two-note song, an orchestra of A's and B-flats.

Dori could almost picture her cousin running through the woods, branches and briars tearing at her skin, insects trailing behind her like beads of sweat.

Dori kissed the top of Emily's head, which smelled of smoke. Her back stiffened. Circling the bedroom, she sniffed the air. She could feel the baby's heartbeat, the birdlike throb of her breath against her neck.

Dori stood in the hallway a moment. The baby's lips parted with a bubble blown against her throat. Her tiny fingers clasped at nothing.

Dori's body ached with tension. She carried Emily downstairs and gazed through the screen door at the mysterious glow of the lime-green camper. She pictured it ablaze, an orange torch against a black backdrop. Grabbing a flashlight from the cereal cupboard, she ventured outside, her feet sinking into the spongy grass.

A siren wailed in the distance. Dori pointed her flashlight at the open camper door. "Willa?" she said, her voice unexpectedly harsh. She aimed the beam inside at the dirty green cupboards, clothes, the empty space. Nobody home. On top of the bed in a heap were the stolen diner goods, a jumble of glass and molded metal.

She raced back into the house, heart pounding. She sat with Emily in the living room and rocked her back and forth. Her hands and feet had grown cold, and she couldn't remember the last time she'd felt this lonely.

When Tom finally pulled into the driveway, Dori threw open the door. He stepped out of the car, red hair matted to his forehead, his exhausted eyes on her.

"Is she here?" he asked hopefully.

"No." Dori shook her head. They stood in stiffened silence, separated by the frosty yard light, the baby heating her chest like a hot plaster.

"I'll go out again, soon as I've had some coffee."

"I'm coming with you."

She strapped the baby in back, and they headed for the dump. They circled the Hurryback Cafe twice, then tried the corner store. They crawled along curving back roads, their headlights sweeping ahead like bright plumes of breath. Exhaustion tugged at Dori's muscles, her bones. "Let's try the lake," she finally said, and they kept their silence while whitened trees rushed past like busy gremlins.

They spotted her as soon as they pulled into the public lot. Willa was standing at the end of the wharf in her cutoffs and bra. Except for a stray dog, the lakefront was deserted.

Tom reached for the door, but Dori stopped him. "I'll go," she said.

As she approached, Willa felt her footsteps on the wharf and turned around. Dori's shadow looped across the rotten boards, and the moon cast jagged shimmering lines over the center of the lake. Willa swiftly turned around and raised her arms above her head.

"Dori!" Tom cried, but she silenced him with an abrupt wave. Willa had survived far worse—high dives from cliffs and a fiery second story.

She tilted forward, imperceptibly rocking herself off-balance, then fell with grace from the wharf. As she hit the water, it folded her in its black embrace.

The van door slammed; Tom jogged toward Dori, his thinning hair fanning away from his bony face, his jug ears exposed. He held her around the middle as they gazed intently at the gently lapping water. "Aren't you going to do something?" he asked.

"I am." She held her breath. Willa's head popped up, slick as a seal's, several yards away.

Tom waved his arms, but Dori simply made a "W" with her fingers and held it to her cheek. W-cheek, Willa's name-sign. "Willa, Willa."

Willa breathed steadily as, treading water, she considered them. Reluctantly at first, and then more rapidly, she stroked back toward the wharf. She hauled herself out of the water, heavy beads dropping from her like a cloak of nails. And before Dori could catch her breath, Willa was shivering in her arms.

Acknowledgements

"Claybottom Lake" was published in The Worcester Review, won a PEN syndicated Fiction Project Award and was broadcast on National Public Radio's "The Sound of Writing" during the fall of 1992. "The Stuntman's Daughter" was published in The William and Mary Review, Vol. 27 in 1989 (ed. William Clark). "Annabelle" first appeared in Turnstile, Vol. III, No. 1 in 1992 (ed. Mitchell Nauffts). "Americans" first appeared in Turnstile, Vol. I, No. 1 in 1988 (ed. Mitchell Nauffts). "Messages" first appeared in The Nebraska Review, Vol. XVII, No. 2 in 1989 (ed. Richard Duggin). "Corporation Beach" won First Prize in the 1989 New Letters Literary Awards and was published n Vol. 56, No. 1 (ed. James McKinley). "Puddle Tongue" won First Prize in the 1994 Iowa Woman Annual Literary Competition and was published in Vol. 14, No. 2 (ed. Marianne Abel). Also thanks to Centrum Artists in Residence Program and the Virginia Center for the Creative Arts.

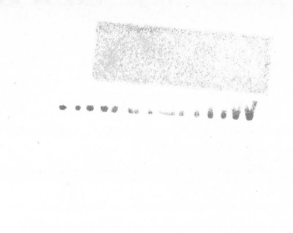